THE BOBBSEY TWINS BOOKS

By Laura Lee Hope

THE BOBBSEY TWINS
AT THE ICE CARNIVAL

To their horror, they were staring at a wild-looking animal

The Bobbsey Twins
at the Ice Carnival

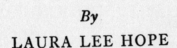

By
LAURA LEE HOPE

Published by
WORLD DISTRIBUTORS (MANCHESTER) LIMITED
LONDON – MANCHESTER
ENGLAND

Heather from Nannie
July 6th 1960.

CONTENTS

CHAPTER I

"I'LL take a box of biscuits, please," said the curly-haired Flossie to her brother Bert. He was the assistant behind the counter in the Bobbsey play store.

"All right," said the boy, handing over a small box. "But don't eat any of them."

Flossie giggled. "Real store men don't tell the ladies not to eat the things they buy."

Bert tried not to laugh. For a moment he had forgotten to be a businesslike grocery assistant. He had on a big white apron which he had borrowed from the cook Dinah, and wore a pencil behind one ear.

"I'll take some salt, too," said blonde Flossie. "And wrap it up very carefully, please, 'cause I've a long way to go."

Both children laughed at that, for the distance Flossie would have to go with her packages was no farther than from the Bobbsey dining-room to the Bobbsey living-room. Here Flossie had built herself a house of four chairs turned upside down and an ironing-board. The ironing-board served as a door!

As the little girl left the store, her twin brother Freddie and Bert's twin, Nan, entered together. Nan stepped aside to let Flossie pass.

"How do you do, Mrs. White?" she asked politely.

7

"Very well, thank you, Mrs. Black," chuckled Flossie. "Isn't it a snowy day?"

"Yes, and the travelling is dreadful," agreed Nan. Then she added in her plain, everyday voice, "Oh, Flossie, do be careful! There's salt spilling from your package all over the rug."

"There's sugar on the rug, too," said Freddie, pointing to a thin white line that stretched from the kitchen door right across the dining-room floor. "I don't want to play store any more," he added. "I want to play fire."

Freddie loved fires and fire-engines better than anything else. He owned a wonderful toy engine, and Mr. Bobbsey often called his little son "Fat Fireman". The boy wandered to the window where he stood looking out sadly.

The day was bleak and wintry. Some of the snow that had fallen during the night had melted, then had frozen again. Everything was coated with ice. The sky was grey and an icy wind played around the house. It rattled the windows and shrieked down the chimneys. Freddie saw a man hurry along the street.

"You can't see his ears," the little boy said aloud. "His big collar covers them up."

It was Saturday morning. Ordinarily the four Bobbsey children would have been off to a favourite coasting hill or skating pond. But this was no ordinary day. For hours the temperature had been around zero. Mrs. Bobbsey, afraid of frost-nipped fingers and toes, had asked the children to amuse themselves within doors. The play store had been fun for a while, but now they were growing tired of it.

"Let's find something else to do," suggested Nan, who was busily sweeping up the trail of sugar and salt. "When Dinah finishes her kitchen cleaning we'll ask her to let us make some candy. How would you like that?"

Before any of them could answer, Freddie whirled from the window, his face shining with excitement.

"I hear a fire-engine!" he cried. "And it's coming this way! It's a real fire, not a play fire. Hurrah! Hurrah!"

The others listened. Sure enough, they could hear the brassy clamour of the bell and the wailing siren as the big truck sped along.

All the children rushed into the front room, calling to their mother and Dinah as they ran. From the windows they could see the fire-engine turn into their street. Wonder of wonders, it stopped before their own door! This was more than Freddie had bargained for.

"Golly, our house isn't on fire!" he cried, bewildered. "What are they stopping here for?"

Bert and Nan rushed to the door and flung it wide open, letting in a blast of bitter wind. From the stairway Mrs. Bobbsey called down to ask what was happening. Dinah ran from the kitchen, wiping her hands on her apron. A fireman leaped from the truck and rushed up to the porch.

"All right, sonny," he said, brushing past Bert. "We'll soon have it out. Where's the fire?"

"We haven't any fire," said Freddie, jumping up and down in his excitement.

"No fire!" The man looked about him angrily. "Then who——"

"No one telephoned from this house, Officer," said Mrs. Bobbsey decidedly. "There's been some mistake."

"I'll say there has," growled the man in uniform. "Another practical joker probably, playing tricks on the department. There's got to be a stop put to this sort of thing."

At that moment Nan saw something from the window. A woman was stumbling across the street, slipping and sliding on the icy pavement. A short coat was flung over her head and shoulders to protect her from the bitter wind. She was shouting wildly to the firemen.

"My house!" Nan heard her cry. "My house is on fire! Oh, hurry! Hurry!"

"It's Mrs. Kape from across the street, Mother," said the girl excitedly.

As the firemen swung into action Mrs. Bobbsey took charge of her own family. She herded the children away from the door and into the warmth of the living-room. At the same time she insisted upon the shivering Mrs. Kape coming inside. Then she led her into the living-room.

"I'll have Dinah make you a cup of tea," she said sympathetically. "What a terrible thing to happen! Have you any idea how the fire started?"

"I think I must have tried to force our furnace too much. It is old and my husband has been meaning for a long time to do something about it. And now this has to happen—and with him away, too! Oh, dear, what shall I do?" cried the unfortunate woman.

From the windows the children watched the firemen at work on Mrs. Kape's home. Suddenly Freddie cried:

"Oh, I can see the flames now! They're in the front of the house!"

"Oo, there's a lot of smoke!" Flossie added.

With a cry the neighbour rushed to the window. "All my suitcases are in the hall. Oh, dear, I must do something!"

"Were you going on a trip, Mrs. Kape?" Nan asked, surprised.

"Yes, I am going up north to meet my husband. He is to be one of the special skaters at the big Ice Carnival there. He really skates beautifully; does all kinds of fancy figures. But now I don't know what I shall do."

"Need this make a difference to your plans?" asked Mrs. Bobbsey. "My husband and I will be glad to take charge of things for you here until you get back," she offered.

"You are kind, and I do thank you, but you see you don't quite understand. In the suitcases are the skating costumes my husband ordered and must have for the carnival. If they are destroyed there will be no time to have others made."

As she said this, the Bobbsey children looked at one another. Mrs. Kape took her coat up again and turned to the door.

"I must go back to the house," she said hurriedly. "Perhaps I can save something."

"You better stay here. I'll go," offered Bert.

Before anyone could stop him the boy had snatched a leather coat and knitted cap from the closet and darted out into the wintry gale.

"What a dreadful wind!" said Mrs. Kape, shivering in spite of the warmth of the Bobbsey house. "It will spread the flames to other buildings, I am afraid. Oh, what a terrible, terrible thing to happen!"

"Please try not to worry," Mrs. Bobbsey said soothingly. "Soon they will have the flames under control.

Drink some of Dinah's hot tea," she added, as the cook came to the doorway. "I am sure it will make you feel better."

Thoughtful Nan drew up a comfortable chair for the guest while Flossie took the tea-tray from Dinah and placed it on a low table at her elbow.

"Thank you so much. You are very kind," she said gratefully.

Meanwhile, slipping and sliding across the street, head bent against the icy wind, Bert finally reached the burning building. No one had noticed him. Then one of the firemen, who was carrying the ice-covered hose, saw him and ordered him away. Bert slipped past the man and ran around to the back of the house.

One of the windows here was broken. Bert raised the sash and was inside in a flash. A gust of black smoke met him and made his eyes water. He brushed a hand across them impatiently and looked about him.

"This must be a library," he thought. "I wonder if that door goes into the hall."

There were shelves of books along one wall and a writing-desk as well as several easy chairs. It would be a shame if these things should burn up. There was no sign of flames here yet but there was a steady hum and crackle from the front of the house.

In a moment the smoke curled more heavily under and around the cracks of the door. Bert flung open the door and stumbled into a wave of great heat. He could see nothing burning, but the smoke was stifling. It got into his nose and down his throat, strangling him.

"There are the bags," he decided, looking towards the front door.

Before him he could see the piled-up suitcases.

Their shapes were vague and shadowy through the smoke haze. He must get to them quickly.

Bert found a muffler which had been stuffed into a pocket of his coat. He pulled it out and pressed it against his nose and mouth. Shutting his eyes, he made a swift dash for the suitcases.

CHAPTER II

COUGHING and spluttering beneath his muffler, Bert finally reached the bags. Quickly he grabbed up two of them and started for the front door. Suddenly he was stopped by a big man in a rubber coat and helmet. The boy had not seen the figure in the hall.

"Where do you think you're going?" asked the fireman in a deep voice. "Those things don't belong to you, do they? Now hustle out of here before you get hurt."

Bert didn't want to go without the suitcases. And he didn't want to get smoke in his throat by talking. So he just mumbled something.

"Can't hear you," said the fireman, taking the boy by the shoulders and pushing him.

As Bert stumbled through the heat and smoke he thought of other adventures when he had had to convince grown-ups that he was doing a worth-while thing and not just getting in their way. They never gave a fellow credit for having common sense, he thought!

As a matter of fact, the Bobbsey twins were always having adventures of one sort or another. Most people who knew them agreed that Bert and Nan, the elder pair, had an unusual amount of common sense for their age. Perhaps this was because of the habit both

Nan and Bert had of looking after the little twins, Flossie and Freddie.

The children lived with Mr. and Mrs. Bobbsey in Lakeport, where Mr. Bobbsey was in the lumber business. The family was loyally served by good-natured Dinah, the coloured cook, and her husband, Sam, who was chauffeur and general handyman about the place.

Sharing the twins' adventures whenever it was possible were their two dogs: Snap, the old one, gentle, friendly and kind; and young Waggo, who was full of pep and playfulness and always ready for whatever romp was at hand.

Right now Bert had little time to think of dogs or anything else as he was being pushed through the smoke-filled hall of the burning house. Just as he reached the front door, something happened to him. A stream of water, playing upon the fire in the front room, was turned suddenly. It sprayed him with icy water.

"You'll get worse than a dousing if you don't hustle," the fireman warned him. "Better get home now and into dry clothes, my lad, before you freeze stiff."

Bert struggled in the man's grasp and wrenched himself free.

"Please help me get these suitcases out," he pleaded. "I promised Mrs. Kape I would. It's important."

The fireman looked undecided for a moment, then he said gruffly, "All right, I'll help you get them out. Though what's in 'em to make such a fuss about is beyond me. Must be full of gold and diamonds."

"No, only skating costumes," said Bert, panting as he shouldered one of the heavy grips.

The fireman stared for a moment, then shrugged his shoulders. "Nothing is important enough for a person to rush into a burning building," he said.

As Bert reached the icy porch and set down the suitcase, he saw a man slip along the driveway towards the back of the house. He had flaming red hair and bushy eyebrows. There was something sneaky in his manner that caught Bert's attention. When the fireman returned with the last of the grips Bert mentioned the man to him and the latter promised to keep a look-out for the fellow.

"Probably some neighbour trying to do a rescue job," he said. "But if he's a thief he won't get far, never fear. We'll see to that."

By this time Bert was so cold that his teeth were chattering. The bitter wind cut through him like so many knives. He started for home, eager to be rid of his wet, fast-freezing clothes and to toast himself before an open fire.

Meanwhile things had been happening in the Bobbsey's house. Twice Freddie had tried to run outside, to be caught by his mother just in time.

Nan and Flossie, watching the progress of the fire from the window, were worrying about Bert. So they were overjoyed when they saw their brother come out of Mrs. Kape's house carrying the heavy suitcase.

Flossie jumped up and down joyfully. In her excitement she grasped one of the long, heavy curtains, pulling it down on top of herself and Nan! The two girls became so entangled they fell to the floor, unable to get out of the folds.

"Children, what are you doing?" cried Mrs. Bobbsey, rushing to the rescue. "Dinah, do help me get them out!" she called to the cook.

"Yas'm, I'll help yo' get 'em out," said Dinah. "But de question is, how did dey-all git in? Ef yo' don't stop wrigglin', Miss Flossie," she added, "I ain't never gwine to be able to tell which end of yo' is which. Yo' all is just got to stay dere de rest of yo' nat'ral life."

At this threat Flossie became as still as a mouse. At last they were able to find out where the curtains ended and Flossie began. A very red-faced little girl finally appeared and begged her mother's and Nan's pardon for being so clumsy.

"I got so excited I forgot I had hold of the curtain," she explained.

At that moment Freddie called from the upstairs hall. "Here comes Bert. He's got a fireman with him and a lot of suitcases. I guess maybe the cases belong to you, Mrs. Kape."

Everyone crowded into the hall as Bert entered. He dropped the cases and gave a great sigh. He was followed by the man carrying still more of the suitcases.

"The fire's out, ma'am," he said, addressing Mrs. Kape. "This brave lad here," with a hand on Bert's shoulder, "risked his life to rescue some of your property. He's a good boy and no mistake. I only wish I had one like him."

Nan and the little twins glowed with pride at this praise of their brother. Freddie, running downstairs to get closer to his hero, slipped in the little pool of icy water that was dripping from Bert's clothing. Down he came with a plop in the middle of the puddle!

"Oh, dear, what next!" cried Mrs. Bobbsey.

She shook her head over Freddie's plight and sent the little boy upstairs to change into a dry suit. As soon as Bert had been thanked by Mrs. Kape, he, too, was sent to take a hot bath and change into other clothing.

While Dinah mopped up the wet patches in the hall Mrs. Kape asked the fireman about the extent of the damage to her home. "Is it very bad?"

"Well, it's not so bad, ma'am, all things considered," the man replied. "We managed to keep most of the damage to the front of the house. I'm afraid your living-room and part of the hall are pretty well wrecked. If you have insurance——"

"Oh, yes, we carry insurance enough to cover the damage, I'm positive. But the thing is, will I be able to live in the house? Is the furnace all right, do you think?"

The fireman shook his head. "It's impossible to have heat in the house, ma'am," he said. "There'll be no living in it for a while, I'm afraid."

"Oh, dear, then I don't know what I'll do," sighed Mrs. Kape.

Mrs. Bobbsey interrupted her. "You must stay here with us, of course," she said. "We have room and we'll be glad to have you. Won't we, girls?" she asked her daughters.

"Oh, yes!" said Flossie with an excited bounce. "We never have fire ladies visit us."

"You can tell us all about the Ice Carnival," Nan proposed. "I've always wanted to see one. If you will tell us about it, that will be the next best thing," she added.

So it was arranged that Mrs. Kape was to stay with the Bobbseys until it should be time for her to leave for Fairy Lake. That was where the great Ice Carnival was to be held.

The poor lady was very grateful to the Bobbsey

family. They were such good friends in times of need. She was especially pleased about Bert having saved the suitcases and their precious contents.

"You must have a reward," she told the boy. "Now don't say 'no', because I have made up my mind. I'll think of something."

When Mr. Bobbsey came home that night he was very much surprised at the turn of events. He greeted Mrs. Kape kindly and listened with great interest and sympathy to the story of the fire. Bert's part in the doing, as related by Freddie and Flossie, lost nothing in the telling, you may be sure.

"Well, I see that my son is something of a hero," said Mr. Bobbsey with a teasing look at Bert. "But seriously, I am very glad you were able to help out, son," he added, "and I hope you will always be as prompt to help anyone in distress."

Bert protested that he really had done nothing to make a fuss about. After dinner was over and they were all gathered in the living-room Mr. Bobbsey drew a paper from his pocket.

"I just remembered seeing some pictures of Fairy Lake," he said to Mrs. Kape. "It really is a beautiful place, isn't it?"

"As beautiful as its name," the woman nodded, accepting the paper. The children gathered around her. "It really is like fairyland. Coloured lights are strung out across the lake and others twinkle among the trees. It's hard to imagine anything lovelier. Then the music—oh, it's all enchanting. No one can really describe it. It has to be seen—and heard."

"I want to go!" cried Flossie, clapping her hands. "Mother, Daddy, can't we?"

"I'm afraid not, Fat Fairy," said Mr. Bobbsey,

using his pet name for Flossie. "Even though we might pretend it's named after you, Fairy Lake is a long way off, you know. I guess we shall have to look at the pictures and imagine we have seen it."

"Perhaps Mrs. Kape will write to us after she gets there and tell us all about it," Mrs. Bobbsey suggested with a smile.

"Indeed I will," their neighbour promised, adding gratefully, "That would be a very little return for all you have done for me. Now I wonder if I couldn't——"

"Couldn't what?" the children prompted, as she paused.

"Oh, nothing. I guess I was just thinking out loud. And now," smiling at her eager young audience, "would you like me to tell you all about Fairy Lake and the carnival and the part my husband is going to take in it?"

Saying that they would like nothing better, the children grouped themselves close to the story-teller. They listened, enchanted, to her tales of Fairy Lake until Mrs. Bobbsey came in with the announcement that it was past their bedtime.

When the children had gone upstairs, Mrs. Kape asked permission to put in a long-distance call to her husband at Fairy Lake. So it happened that Nan, passing through the hall above on the way to her own room, heard the woman say:

"Oh, Hugh, I hoped you'd agree! That will be a grand reward for Bert."

CHAPTER III

WHAT was to be the "grand reward for Bert"?

Nan was so surprised that she stood still and listened without in the least meaning to eavesdrop. However, there was nothing further to hear. Mrs. Kape talked to her husband for a few minutes, then said good-bye. She went back into the living-room where Mr. and Mrs. Bobbsey were still sitting before the fire.

"I wonder what she meant," the girl said to herself.

Nan was thoughtful as she continued on to her own room. Mrs. Kape's words had sounded very exciting. As the girl slipped into bed she thought of all the nice things that might happen to her twin. It was hard not to share her thoughts with him and harder still to wait until morning to hear what the woman would have to tell.

Finally, Nan fell asleep and dreamed that a lovely new sports car suddenly drew up before the Bobbsey door. On its side was painted in big white letters:

A GRAND REWARD FOR BERT

The next thing Nan knew a shaft of bright sunlight was streaming across her face. It was morning. As she reached for her woolly robe and slipped her feet into bedroom slippers she was surprised to see that Flossie was already up and dressed.

"Br-r, it's cold!" said Nan, and rushed across to put down the window. "What are you up so early for, Flossie? Did Dinah call us?"

"No, I just felt like getting up," said the little girl. "And I'm not cold 'cause I have on my snow suit."

"Well, it looks pretty silly to me," said Nan, shivering as she hurried into her clothes. "A snow suit isn't meant to wear in the house, you know."

"But I'm not in the house," said Flossie placidly.

Nan stared. "Then where are you, please?" she demanded.

"I'm at Fairy Lake and so's my dolly. I'm dressing her in her snow suit, too," said Flossie. "In just a few minutes we're going out on the ice."

Nan finished fastening her dress and put on a soft, blue woolly sweater that Aunt Sallie Pry had sent her for Christmas. Mention of Fairy Lake brought back with a rush all her happy thoughts of the night before. Now, perhaps, she would find out what Mrs. Kape's reward for Bert would be! On the way to the door, Nan paused to give Flossie a hug.

"Better get some breakfast before you go skating on Fairy Lake," she suggested gaily.

The little girl agreed that this might be a good idea. She trotted along at Nan's side down to the dining-room, her dolly clutched tightly to her chest.

This doll was the delight of Flossie's life. It had come to her at Christmastime and with it a trunk of its very own. It held several changes of pretty costumes. Among these was a skating outfit, complete from the flaring skirt and the snug, fur-bordered jacket, to the little shoes fitted with a pair of tiny ice-skates. No wonder Flossie was eager to dress her dolly for a morning on Fairy Lake.

The rest of the family, including their guest, were just sitting down to breakfast when the girls appeared. Everyone said good morning.

"Ho, look at Flossie," teased Freddie. "She thinks she's an Eskimo, eating in her outdoor suit."

Mrs. Bobbsey checked him from saying more, but suggested that Flossie might find the snow suit a little warm for the inside of the house.

"Besides, it might be hard to eat in," smiled Mr. Bobbsey. "Take off the suit, Fat Fairy, and come and get some of Dinah's good cereal. It's a little extra delicious this morning."

"All right, but I'm not going to undress my dolly. She likes to be warm," said Flossie, pulling off her own heavy clothing.

The family was about to begin breakfast when someone noticed that Freddie was missing.

"He was here just a minute ago," Nan said.

"I think he went to clean his fire-engine. He said he got it dirty fighting the fire yesterday," grinned Bert.

The little boy was sent for and returned a moment later clutching his toy fire-engine jealously.

"Freddie, you can't bring your toys to the table," said Mrs. Bobbsey with a patient sigh. "Put it in the other room, dear, and come right back. We are all waiting for you."

When they were finally settled, Mrs. Kape spoke at last of the subject that was nearest Nan's heart— the reward for Bert.

"As you know, I made a long-distance call to my husband last night," she began. "He is staying at an hotel which is owned by his brother. I told him how kind you have been to me and he is very, very grateful, of course. At first he was worried about the skating costumes. Then I told him that, thanks to Bert's quick thinking and acting, they hadn't been damaged at all."

Nan paused with one of Dinah's hot biscuits halfway to her mouth and regarded Mrs. Kape with lively interest. In a moment she would know just what the grand reward was to be!

"I'm sure Bert doesn't want any reward, Mrs. Kape," Mrs. Bobbsey interrupted quickly.

"But if we could do something for him that would give us great pleasure, too, surely you would not refuse." Their guest leaned forward and regarded Mr. and Mrs. Bobbsey earnestly. "Both Mr. Kape and myself have set our hearts on having Bert spend a week with us at Fairy Lake. Please say that he may go—that is, if he wants to," the woman added with a smiling glance at Bert.

"If I want to!" cried the boy eagerly. "Why, I can't think of a thing I'd like better. It's swell of you to ask me. Only," with an uncertain glance at his parents, "Mother and Dad are right, of course. I don't deserve any reward."

"If you really want to go for a week to Fairy Lake, I guess it can be managed," said Mr. Bobbsey, who had exchanged an understanding look with his wife. "I think it is very generous and kind of Mr. and Mrs. Kape to suggest it," he added.

So it was settled to everyone's satisfaction. The little twins and Nan were as happy over Bert's good fortune as the boy himself. All that remained was to find out just when Mrs. Kape expected to start and to make sure that the boy would be ready in plenty of time to go with her.

"I must attend to the insurance and see about repairs to my home," said Mrs. Kape. "That will keep me in town for several days."

Mrs. Bobbsey thought she could get Bert all he needed for the trip in that time. Daddy said he would drive the two ladies to town first thing the next morning and would do all he could to help Mrs. Kape get her business affairs straightened out. Nothing could be done that day, of course, as it was Sunday.

After breakfast the twins put on their heaviest clothes and went across the street to inspect the damaged house. Since some of the windows had been broken a policeman was stationed there to keep away anybody who might take things. There was a crowd of youngsters around the house. As the Bobbsey children approached it, they saw the policeman reach out and grasp one of the youngsters by his coat.

"No, you don't, my fine friend," he said. "How many times have I got to be tellin' you to keep away from the house? Once more and I'll run you into the station, that I will."

He gave the lad a final shake and let him go. The boy turned around, scowling, and his glance fell on the Bobbseys.

"There's the fellow you want to run in," he charged, pointing straight at Bert. "I bet he set the fire on purpose."

There was a gasp among the group of children, most of whom were friends of the Bobbsey twins. One or two of them cried:

"For shame, Danny Rugg! You know Bert never would set a house on fire."

Following the direction of Danny's pointing finger, the officer saw Bert and grinned broadly. He even touched his cap to the lad as a sign of friendly feeling.

"Now I know you're crazy," he said to Danny Rugg. "It's all over town how Bert Bobbsey rushed into the burnin' house to rescue some of the owners' prized belongings. He wouldn't set fire to the house, would he now, and then risk his life in such a fashion?"

"You bet he would if he thought it was going to make a hero out of him," said the unpleasant boy. "He likes being a hero enough to set a dozen houses afire."

There was another gasp from the crowd of youngsters and Bert stepped forward with clenched fists.

"That's just about enough from you!" he said to the bully.

"Yeah, and what do you think you're going to do?" jeered Danny, backing away nevertheless from Bert's clenched fists.

"Now, now, none of that, lads," said the policeman soothingly. "Can't have any fights in the street, you know, or I'll have to be runnin' you both in."

Danny grinned tauntingly at Bert. "So now you can be a hero all you like. You've got a policeman to protect you," he jeered.

Again Bert stepped forward and again was stopped by the officer's hand on his arm.

"Well, I'll be seeing you," said Danny. "So long till next time."

He waved airily and turned around, meaning to

go off in triumph. But at that moment loyal little Freddie raised his sled cord and caught the bully about the ankles, tripping him neatly.

Up went Danny's legs and down went Danny. He slid on his back along the icy ground while the crowd of children laughed and cheered.

The first thing the mean boy saw when he pulled himself to his feet was the broad grin on Bert's face. He scowled and hobbled off while the youngsters hooted with laughter.

With Danny gone, the others gathered around Bert. They showered him with questions about the fire and his part in it. Then Flossie told them of Bert's invitation to spend a week at Fairy Lake. Of course they had to hear about that, too.

"I wish you all were going," Bert said. "But I'll send you postcards, anyway, and tell you everything when I get back."

Meanwhile Nan suggested having a Fairy Lake of their own.

"The Lakeport pond must be frozen over. Let's get our skates and go down there," she proposed. "We can make up some fancy steps."

"And I'll take my fire-engine, in case there's a fire," said Freddie.

"I'll make my dolly do a special dance," added Flossie.

"I'll bring my portable radio so we can even have music," said Charlie Mason, who was Bert's best friend.

Someone shouted, "Well, what are we waiting for? Let's go!"

Off they went in a happy throng, leaving the

policeman to look after the house. How he wished he were a lad again and could spend a happy time on the neighbourhood skating pond.

After that, "Fairy Lake" became a favourite meeting place with the younger children of Lakeport. Every afternoon after school they met and practiced fancy twirls and glides. Finally Flossie declared they must be almost good enough to go in a real carnival.

Bert had to interrupt these pleasant afternoons to go shopping with his mother and Nan. This seemed to him to be a complete waste of time.

"What do I have to go shopping for?" he protested. "I have a ski suit and a pair of skis and skates already. What more do I need?"

"I don't know why Mother bothers with you," Nan said once when Bert had been more than usually balky. "She might just as well try to dress a mule!"

The thought of a mule in one of Bert's suits made the boy laugh. So everything was peaceful once more.

At last all the shopping had been done. Bert's cases were packed and placed beside Mrs. Kape's in the lower hall. Tickets had been bought for the early morning train.

The boy was so excited that he could scarcely sleep at all that night. He dropped into a broken slumber at last, however, but he was up again with the first hint of daylight.

'This is the day, the big day!" he said to himself.

As he jumped out of bed he was amazed to see snow on the floor. Where the window was open it had drifted in, covering the rug beneath with a thin frosty blanket.

Bert ran to the window and looked out. The snow

was falling steadily. The boy couldn't see across the street! A thick white carpet lay on the ground. There were no wagon or car tracks anywhere.

"Looks like a blizzard," thought Bert. "A fine day to start for Fairy Lake! Oh," he groaned, "maybe we can't go."

CHAPTER IV

THE BLIZZARD

FEARFUL that the trip would be called off, Bert nevertheless dressed himself in his travelling-suit. Before the rest of the family got up he was outside helping Sam to clear the paths and the drive. The snow was so deep it was very hard work.

"Yo' bettah come in heah," called Dinah after a while, "lessen yo' want to spoil yo' good clothes. Anyhow, breakfast is ready."

At the table there was a great deal of talk back and forth about whether Mrs. Kape and Bert should start. The storm was getting worse each minute.

"I want to go to the station," said Freddie, "and see the train in the snow."

"I want to go, too," spoke up Flossie.

Now Mr. Bobbsey had not planned to take any of the children, but finally he decided it might be a lark. So pretty soon they all piled into the car and started.

Steam collected on the windscreen and the wiper kept up a steady clicking as it strove to clear the view. Mr. Bobbsey had all he could do to keep to the road.

They reached the station without mishap, however, and found that there were still five minutes left to wait before the train would pull in. The five minutes seemed very long to Bert.

"I wish you were going with me," he said as the train whistle shrieked. He was beginning to realize that he would miss his family very much.

Amid a good deal of excitement, hand wavings and instructions from the little twins and Nan, Mrs. Kape and Bert finally got aboard. Mr. Bobbsey went inside with them to see that they were comfortable and to leave with Mrs. Kape the magazines and chocolate he had bought in the station waiting-room.

As the train started to move the children ran along the snowy platform beside it, waving and calling messages to Bert. It was doubtful if he heard anything they said for the windows were shut and the train made a great noise in getting under way.

"Good-bye," said his lips, then he began motioning with his hands.

"What did he mean?" asked Flossie.

"I think he wants us to be sure to remember to feed Snap and Waggo," replied Nan.

Freddie laughed. "Bert did look as if he were making believe he was chewing a bone."

Mr. Bobbsey was silent as they drove towards home. Even during the short time since they had been away the snow had piled up deeper than ever. The wind had risen, also, and beat the white flakes against the windscreen so that it was impossible to see more than a few feet ahead.

"If this gets any worse, we'll be having a real blizzard," he said.

Just as he spoke, a taxicab skidded around the corner. It turned crazily in the heavily rutted snow and bore down directly towards the Bobbsey car!

For a breathless minute it looked as if there would be a crash. Both the taxi driver and Mr. Bobbsey acted quickly, however, driving their cars hard over to opposite sides of the road. There was a scraping of bumpers and a jar as both vehicles came to a standstill.

Mr. Bobbsey opened the door. Squinting against the blinding snow, he shouted to the driver of the taxicab.

"Sorry. Couldn't see you in time. Any harm done?" he asked.

The driver had been peering from the lowered window at what he could see of the bumper that had been hit.

"Just a little bent, sir. No damage to speak of," he reported.

Here the passenger of the taxi took a hand. He lowered the window on his side and called across to the Bobbseys.

"Hallo! Don't you know me? I'm your neighbour, Hugh Kape."

"That's Mrs. Kape's husband!" cried Flossie, staring hard.

"What can he be doing in Lakeport?" Nan wondered. "He's supposed to be at Fairy Lake at the carnival."

Meanwhile, the children's father had stepped out of the car and was talking to the two men. After a moment Mr. Kape paid the taximan and got into the Bobbsey's car. The twins and Nan squeezed over in one corner to make room for him.

"I'm afraid I'm crowding you," said their unexpected passenger, but the children replied politely that there was plenty of room.

"We thought you were at Fairy Lake," spoke up Flossie.

"So I was and, from what your father tells me, I guess it would have been just as well if I'd stayed there," said Mr. Kape ruefully. "I must have left the station just as my wife and your brother got aboard. It's all my own fault for not sending a telegram, though," he added quickly. "I'd intended to, but then I thought I'd get home almost as quickly as the wire and so came on myself."

"As long as you are here you must plan to stay with us," said Mrs. Bobbsey kindly. "We can give you the room your wife has had. I'm afraid your own house isn't very livable just now," she added.

"Yes. That's what I really came home about. I wanted to find out for myself just how badly the house was damaged," Mr. Kape explained. "Is it bad?" he asked.

"Well, there it is," said Mr. Bobbsey, as he swung into their own street. "We have had the broken windows boarded up and the pipes drained so that everything is safe inside. Your wife thought it would be better not to make the repairs until your return from the Ice Carnival."

"Very likely," said Mr. Kape, adding thoughtfully, "I suppose it was foolish of me to come down. You have been very kind indeed to help us. I'll just hop off here and inspect my place."

"I'm afraid you'll find it pretty dreary," suggested Mrs. Bobbsey, "so please don't stay long. Come to our place in a few minutes."

"Thank you, but I really think I should go to an hotel," he replied. "The Kape family has been trouble enough to you as it is."

Of course none of the Bobbseys would agree to this. Mr. Bobbsey put an end to the discussion by pointing out that the snow was getting so deep that most of the roads into town would be blocked anyway. So it was agreed the man would come, and Mr. Bobbsey waited a few minutes while Mr. Kape took a quick look at his burned home.

"It's a blizzard, and no mistake," said Mr. Bobbsey as he paused at his own porch to let his family out. "If they don't get the snow-ploughs working pretty soon we'll all be snowed in."

None of the children could remember ever having seen so much snow. Driven by the wind, it stung their faces and half-blinded them as they stumbled towards the shelter of the house. They were very glad when Dinah opened the door and let them into the warm hall which smelled deliciously of the soup she was preparing for their luncheon.

"Yo' all looks like a lot of Santa Clauses," said the kindly servant, pushing the door shut against the driving wind. "It sho' am snowin' fit to kill outside. I hopes Master Bert gets through to Fairy Lake all right."

Nan looked hard at Dinah. "Why shouldn't he get through?" she demanded quickly.

"No reason in de world, honey chile," said Dinah, "lessen dat train he's on done git itself stuck in a snowdrift."

"Oh, I don't think the snow is as bad as all that," said Nan. "It can't be."

However, Bert's twin was to remember Dinah's words many times in the hours that followed. Again and again she went to the window, staring out into the solid whiteness.

"Oh, dear," she said to herself, "it would be dreadful if Bert's train should get stopped miles and miles from a town."

Her mother and father and Mr. Kape were worried too. After lunch Mr. Bobbsey tried to put a message through to the station through which the train bearing Mrs. Kape and Bert was due to pass soon, but found this impossible. A worried operator reported that the storm had reached blizzard proportions along the line. Already the damage was considerable. Wires were down and roads blocked but the railroads were still operating, though a long way behind their regular time.

"Suppose I tell you children about the programme for the Ice Carnival," suggested Mr. Kape, even though he too was concerned about his wife and Bert.

In spite of her worry, Nan listened as eagerly as the little twins. The skater told them about the preparations that were going forward to make this carnival "the very best ever".

"At night the coloured lights across the lake are so bright one can see everything almost as well as if it were daytime," he said.

"And are the costumes very pretty? As nice as my dolly's?" asked Flossie, holding up her precious skating doll for Mr. Kape to see.

"Yes, almost as nice as that," said their guest, examining the pretty toy. "Some of the costumes are decorated with tiny lights of their own," he went on, "so that when the skaters do their fancy figures they look like a lot of fireflies dancing out over the ice."

"Oh, it must be beautiful. I do wish we could see it," Nan said longingly.

"I wish so, too," said Mr. Kape. Then he added impulsively, "And why can't you, anyway? Why

don't you all come up with me to Fairy Lake when I
go? How about it, Mrs. Bobbsey?"

The children were too surprised to say anything
for a moment. They just stared at the skater with
wide-open eyes. Then Flossie ran to her father, who
had just come into the room, and slipped her chubby
hand into his.

"Did you hear what Mr. Kape said, Daddy?" she
demanded excitedly. "He asked us all to go with him
to Fairy Lake."

Over Flossie's head Mr. Bobbsey looked at Mr.
Kape and the latter smiled.

"Why not?" he said. "If you can spare the time
from business and the children can get off from
school for a short winter holiday Mrs. Kape and I
would like nothing better than to have you with us at
the lake. Come, what do you say?"

"Oh, Daddy, let's!" begged Freddie, rushing over
also. "Please say we can go!"

"Think of all the fancy steps we could learn," said
Flossie, skipping happily about the room. "We would
skate all day long, wouldn't we, Nan?"

"It would be wonderful, Daddy! Oh, don't you
think we might be able to go?" begged the older
girl.

"Now wait a minute. Not so fast!" said Mr.
Bobbsey. "This is the sort of thing that takes thinking over, you know. I can't possibly give a yes or no
answer right now."

"But you *will* think about it, Daddy?" Nan urged
her father.

"Yes, I can promise that much, and I'll talk with
your mother."

"Hip-hip-hooray," shouted Freddie, prancing

about the room joyfully. "We're going to Fairy Lake, we're going to Fairy Lake——"

"Not so fast," warned Mr. Bobbsey again. "I've made no promises, remember. I'll think it over, but your mother must be the one to decide."

So the rest of the day passed, with the question of a possible trip to Fairy Lake not answered. When the children went to bed that night the snow still fell. In the morning there was a swirling white curtain outside their windows. As they came to the dining-room Nan asked:

"Have you heard anything about Bert, Daddy?"

Mr. Bobbsey raised his hand and gestured towards the radio, which was tuned to a news broadcast.

"Conditions are serious," a voice was reporting. "Roads are blocked, many bus services have stopped running altogether. Train schedules all over the region have been interfered with. There is a report that the Grayson Flyer, the new streamlined beauty, which was carrying many skaters and their friends to the big Ice Carnival at Fairy Lake, has been halted by heavy drifts——"

The voice went on to report news from other sections, but the Bobbseys had heard enough. Daddy snapped off the radio and turned a grave face to his family.

"I hope the snow stops soon," he said, "or the situation may be very bad."

Freddie could see how worried his family was about Bert. He was worried too, but his face brightened as he thought of something that he could do to help. No one noticed when he slipped from the table with a murmured "Excuse me" and tiptoed to his room.

Down he came a few minutes later, dressed in his woolly snow suit and carrying a toy snow shovel. Nan heard the front door open and close quietly. Without saying anything to the rest of the family, she went to see where her brother was.

"Freddie out in this snow!" she said to herself. "The drifts are dreadful! Some of them must be over his head. He might fall into one and be smothered."

Quickly Nan put on her heavy coat. A pair of Bert's boots were in the hall closet so she pulled these on, then crammed a heavy cap over her dark hair.

Opening the door, she bent her head against the wind and snow that greeted her. She looked around for her little brother but could not see him. Then she called loudly but there was no answer.

"Freddie! Freddie! Where are you?" she cried.

CHAPTER V

ALAS for Freddie! As he was busy with the shovel, he suddenly had lost his footing and plunged head-first into a deep snowdrift! He was almost buried, all that remained showing being his boots.

"Oh, oh," cried Nan, darting forward to rescue him.

Slipping and sliding, the girl pushed through the heavy snow. As she reached the spot where her little brother had gone in, her foot struck against something that was certainly not Freddie. She paid little attention to this at the time, for her brother was kicking his feet wildly. He hadn't smothered!

Nan grasped the boot which came off in her hand. But Freddie did not budge.

"Oh, dear, I must get him out or he *will* smother to death," thought Nan, now really alarmed.

Just at this point, however, Freddie pushed out one of his arms. Nan seized it and tugged with all her might, this time with good results.

Gasping and spluttering, blind and half-choked, the little boy was dragged from the snow. Nan brushed the clinging stuff from his nose and mouth. He blinked his eyes to get the lashes free.

"Whatever were you trying to do?" Nan scolded as she led him back to the house.

"I was trying to shovel a path so we could start for Fairy Lake!" the little boy replied.

"Sam will do all the shovelling that needs to be done around here," said Nan.

The little fellow turned obediently towards the house, but before he reached the door he suddenly remembered something he had meant to tell Nan.

"When I fell, I fell *on* something," he said. "It was hard and it felt as if it had handles on it."

This reminded Nan of the object her foot had struck against when she was trying to pull Freddie from the drift. She went back to look for it. After some slipping and floundering about, she finally located the hidden object.

It was not easy to get it out of the deep drift. Finally, with her little brother's help, she managed to do so at last. The two children pulled the heavy snow-covered article up on to the porch, brushed the white flakes from it and discovered—one of Bert's suitcases!

"It must have been forgotten in the excitement yesterday morning. It was never put in the car at all," said Nan in dismay. "Won't Bert be mad when he finds this out!"

When the children showed Mrs. Bobbsey what they had found in the snow, she felt very bad indeed. All the things her son needed most for the trip were in that suitcase.

"If only there were some way of getting it to him," she said. "But until the snow stops we are helpless as if we were all at the North Pole. We can't even get a message through to him."

While Nan was trying to think of something to say that might comfort her mother, Flossie called from the window, "There's a man coming up the front path. I think it's a perliceman but I can't tell, 'cause he's all covered with snow like Santa Claus."

Mrs. Bobbsey opened the door. Sure enough, there stood a policeman.

"Come inside, please," she invited.

"I'd get snow all over your rugs, ma'am," said the officer with a shake of his head. "If it's all the same to you I'll stay outside. I've come about the Kapes' house across the street," he added.

"It hasn't caught on fire again, has it?" asked Flossie, running forward.

"Whoops! I'll go and get my fire-engine!" said Freddie, and started up the stairway.

"Hush, children!" said Mrs. Bobbsey. Then to the policeman, she added, "I hope your news isn't very bad. The Kapes have had trouble enough."

"This is more for them, I'm afraid, ma'am. You see, one of the boarded-up windows was forced during the night. The house has been ransacked from cellar to attic, and many things stolen."

Hearing voices at the door Mr. Kape and Mr. Bobbsey came forward to find out what was going on. The officer repeated his story for them. The two men decided to go with him to the burned house to see for themselves how much damage had been done and what articles had been taken.

From the window the children watched their father and his companions battle their way across the street until they disappeared in a whirl of snow. While they were wondering who the thief could be Nan suddenly remembered something Bert had told her.

"He said a red-haired man had sneaked around the house suspiciously on the day of the fire. I better tell the policeman about it. Maybe that will help him find the thief."

The men were very cold when they returned from their inspection of the burned house. This time the policeman accepted Mrs. Bobbsey's invitation to come inside. While he sipped a cup of Dinah's hot coffee, he listened with interest to what Nan had to tell about the red-haired man.

"See if you can describe him a little better, miss," he directed. "Did your brother say anything else? The height of the man, or the way he was dressed? Did he have any special marks on him, as you might say?"

Nan tried hard to remember just what Bert had told her. "You see, my brother's eyes were half-blinded with smoke and he couldn't see very well. But he did say that the man didn't seem tall and he was dressed in some kind of shabby clothes like a tramp wears."

The policeman nodded.

"Was there anything else, miss?" he asked.

"I—don't think so. Oh, yes, there was," said Nan, brightening. "Bert said the man had funny eyebrows, very bushy and shaggy and red like his hair."

The officer nodded again and got up, carefully placing his empty cup on the table at his elbow.

"I think I have a line on your man, miss," he said. "The description sounds a lot like a person called Beany Ferris, a slippery fellow, if ever I knew one."

"Do you think he's your man, officer?" asked Mr. Kape.

"He may be, sir. We've had news at headquarters that Beany Ferris is robbing houses somewhere in this locality. This sounds like the kind of a job he would pull. Anyway, we'll keep a look-out for him and be sure and let you know if anything turns up."

As the policeman left he noticed that the storm seemed to be slackening a little.

"About time we had a bit of clear weather," he remarked, pulling his collar up about his ears. "Oh, by the way," he added, turning to Mr. Kape, "I think it might be a good idea, sir, to have a watchman posted at your place for a while—just in case Beany Ferris, or whoever it was, takes a notion to pay a return visit."

"Thanks for the suggestion. I'll have it attended to at once, officer," said Mr. Kape.

"Well, I don't b'lieve it was the red-haired man that was the thief at all," said Flossie as they all turned back to the living-room.

"What do you mean, Fat Fairy?" demanded Mr. Bobbsey. "Have you any other ideas about who might have robbed the Kapes' house?"

"Well, I b'lieve it was Danny Rugg," said the little girl decidedly. "He said he would get even with Bert and with Freddie for tripping him up with the sled rope and maybe this was the way he tried to do it."

No one was inclined to take the little girl's ideas on the robbery very seriously. Nan pointed out that Danny would not be hurting Bert or Freddie by robbing the Kapes, but only the Kapes themselves.

"Besides, I don't think Danny Rugg is as bad as that. He may play mean tricks, but I don't think he'd rob a house," she added.

Flossie was silent, but it was plain that she clung to her own ideas on the subject. Danny Rugg, thought the little girl, was bad and mean enough to do any awful thing!

There was some discussion among them as to who should be chosen to guard the empty house. Various people were suggested but at last it was Dinah's husband, old Sam, who solved the question for them.

"I'se got a friend who's out of work at de present moment," said Sam.

He had been on his way to clear the snow from the path and driveway. He had paused in the doorway of the living-room, twirling an old brown hat nervously.

"He's a honest man, Mr. Bobbsey, sir," he stammered. "There won't nobody get into dat house with him on de job, no, sir!"

"Sounds like a good idea to me," said Mr. Kape. "This friend of yours now," he added, turning to Sam, "could he get on the job right away?"

"Yes, sir, Mr. Kape," said Sam. "If you says de word I'll go off to where he lives dis very minute. He'll be right glad to get de job, sir."

And so it was settled. With the permission of Mr. and Mrs. Bobbsey, Sam set off at once to find his friend, returning a short time later with the largest negro the Bobbseys or Mr. Kape had ever seen. The fellow must have measured at least six-feet-four in his stockinged feet and Freddie insisted that he was as broad across as he was tall!

Elmer Brown, as he was called, seemed delighted with his new job. He assured Mr. Kape and the Bobbseys that nobody would enter the burned house.

Freddie in particular was impressed by the great size of Sam's friend. Later Nan found him arranging his toy soldiers on the broad window-sill of the playroom.

"All these soldiers are Elmer Brown's brothers,"

he explained. "Each one of them is six feet ten inches tall and weighs at least twenty stone!"

Nan laughed and asked what they would do.

"Nobody's going to get into our house with them here to guard it," the little boy boasted.

The next moment in came Waggo, the dog. He wanted to know what was going on, so he put his front paws right up on the window-sill! Down went every one of the brave soldiers flat on his face!

"Bad Waggo!" scolded Freddie.

He chased the dog from the room and set up his Elmer Browns again. In a moment Waggo was back. Before he could do any damage, Freddie pulled him away. Alas! The little boy knocked over every soldier with his elbow!

"I guess my guards aren't very good," the lad decided with a sigh and put his little men back into their box.

The children awoke next day to a new world. Gone were the leaden skies and the falling snow. The sun, shining brightly on a sparkling white blanket, made as pretty a view from their windows as anything they would find at Fairy Lake, Nan was sure. Snow-ploughs were at work and roads were open. Telephone wires had been repaired.

"Now I hope to get a message through and find out about the Grayson Flyer," said Mr. Bobbsey, picking up the instrument just before breakfast.

The children crowded around to hear the report. Before he could call the number, there came a loud banging on the front door. Freddie ran to open it.

There stood Bert Bobbsey!

CHAPTER VI

A HAPPY SURPRISE

WHAT a surprise that was! It was wonderful to know Bert was safe.

The children could scarcely believe at first this was their brother, for they had thought he was miles away. But Bert convinced them that it really was he by hugging them all round, even his father, and demanding breakfast right away.

"I'm starved," he cried. "I had some cereal, toast and milk on the train but it was awful. All the way home I've been thinking of Dinah's muffins and scrambled eggs."

"Yes, sir, Master Bert," said the delighted Dinah, grinning in the doorway. "Yo' jest set right down an' I'll fix yo' some fresh. I'se got some bran muffins an' marmalade, too, case yo' wants some."

"Yum-m, do I!" said Bert. "I'll take anything you have—and quick!"

"Dat's de way I likes to hear yo' talk, boy," said Dinah and turned back to the kitchen, still smiling happily.

While he was eating his second breakfast Bert answered all their questions. The lad was surprised to see Mr. Kape, but said that he was sure Mrs. Kape would be glad to learn that her husband was safe and not lost in a snowdrift somewhere.

46

"She was awfully worried when she telephoned to Fairy Lake and found you were gone," Bert added. "Nobody knew where you were."

"That's right," replied the skater. "I didn't tell anyone my plans. I came away in such a hurry."

"Did you get to Fairy Lake?" asked Nan.

"*I* didn't," said Bert. "I hope Mrs. Kape did. We were stuck in the snow for hours. You should have seen the drifts. The flyer couldn't get through."

"Weren't you scared?" asked Flossie, big-eyed, standing right alongside her brother.

"No, it was kind of fun," said Bert. "Everybody was sure the ploughs would be along and dig us out soon. Sure enough, they did, but it was just about then that I found I'd forgotten to take one of my suitcases. It was the one that had most of my clothes in it."

"We found it in a great big drift that I fell in," Freddie explained.

"Well, I'm glad somebody found it. I hadn't any idea where it was," said Bert, starting on his third muffin. "Mrs. Kape thought probably somebody had picked it up by mistake."

"But you haven't explained why you came home, son," Mr. Bobbsey reminded the boy.

"It was because of the suitcase. I thought there was no use going on to Fairy Lake when most of my clothes were lost or stolen. Um-m, these muffins are good," approved Bert. "Got any more, Dinah?"

"No, sir, Mist' Bert, yo' done eat dem all," said the cook with a laugh.

"Well, then, I'll just have to get along," sighed Bert, pushing back his plate. "So when we found the suitcase was gone," he finished his story, "I took the train home. And here I am."

"And glad we are to see you, dear. We've been very worried about you," said Mrs. Bobbsey, relieved.

The little twins and Nan now told Bert all about the happenings at home since he had left. It included the robbery at the Kapes' house. They were in the midst of this story when the policeman who had visited them the day before rang the front doorbell.

"My brother Bert is home," cried Freddie, opening the door.

The officer was glad to see the boy and questioned him for a while about his experience on the day of the fire. He was eager to get the boy's description of the red-haired man who had acted suspiciously on that day.

Bert could add very little to what Nan had already told, however. All the boy remembered was the fiery red hair, the bushy eyebrows of the suspect, and the fact that he was dressed in shabby clothes.

"Sounds like Beany Ferris, all right," said the officer. "Thought we had the fellow trapped last night, but he gave us the slip and got out of town on a northbound train."

"Maybe he's going to Fairy Lake, too," suggested Flossie.

"He might be after the jewels of the king and queen of the carnival," added Freddie.

The officer laughed and promised to think over the suggestions of the little twins.

"And if we catch Beany Ferris, I'll see that you get the credit," he joked.

Although Bert tried to hide it, Mr. Kape could see that the boy was badly disappointed over his failure to have a holiday at Fairy Lake. The neighbour, determined that the lad must not be cheated out of his reward, had a quiet talk with Mr. and Mrs. Bobbsey.

As a result, the children's father called his family into the living-room and told them some wonderful news. He had decided to give them all a holiday, himself included.

"And where do you think?" he asked.

"Not Fairy Lake?" the children chorused.

Mr. Bobbsey nodded and smiled. "Yes, indeed, Fairy Lake!"

Then there *was* excitement in the house!

In the midst of the hubbub the telephone rang. This time it was long distance. Mrs. Kape was on the other end of the line, speaking from the Hotel Windham at Fairy Lake.

"I am so glad you are safe," she said. "And did Bert get home?"

When told of the boy's arrival, she was relieved. Then Mr. Kape told her all about the Bobbsey's proposed trip to the winter resort. His wife was delighted and promised to make reservations for them at his brother's hotel.

"May I speak to Mrs. Kape before you hang up?" Bert whispered to the man at the telephone.

Mr. Kape handed the instrument to the boy. His wife was very glad to speak to Bert. She had been worried, she told him, for fear she had done the wrong thing in sending him home. Now that things had turned out so well, she felt better about it.

The Bobbsey boy told her of the red-haired man who was suspected of breaking into her home. He asked if she had seen him at all, in or near her place, on the day of the fire.

"I believe I——" Mrs. Kape tried to answer.

Then the line went dead. The only response to Bert's repeated calls was a blank silence.

"That's funny," he said, as Nan came into the hall to see what was the matter. "One minute I was talking to Mrs. Kape and the next minute there just wasn't anything."

"Maybe she hung up," Nan suggested.

"No, it wasn't like that at all. The line just went dead," said Bert, evidently puzzled. "I wanted to hear what she had to say about that red-haired fellow, too."

"It's too bad, but we'll find out when we get there," said Mr. Kape. "So everything is settled about the trip," he added as he and the older twins rejoined the others.

All that remained was to set the time of departure. As Mr. Kape was in a hurry to leave, Mrs. Bobbsey promised to settle affairs at home and get the family ready for the journey at the very earliest possible moment.

"But you children will have to help," she told the twins. "There will be tasks for each one of you—beginning right this minute. Flossie may help Dinah sort the laundry and Nan may help with the mending, while the boys get the big trunk out of the storeroom. Hustle now, all of you!"

The youngsters, glad enough to assist, scurried about. Often they got under each other's feet, and more often they were scolded by Dinah for their mistakes. Nevertheless things were getting done.

Early the next morning Mrs. Bobbsey left to do some shopping. Mr. Kape went into town with Mr. Bobbsey to attend to some matters concerning the

burned house. So it was that the children were alone
in their home with Dinah, when another surprise
happened.

The front door-bell rang and Flossie ran to answer
it. Freddie was close behind her and together the
little twins tugged open the door.

Who should they see, leaning on her cane and
looking half-frozen, but a dear old lady. Their
beloved, but deaf, Aunt Sallie Pry!

"Well, well," she said as the little twins looked at
her in surprise. "Aren't you going to ask me inside?"

"Oh, of—of course, Aunt Sallie, come in," said
Flossie loudly.

"We're awfully glad to see you," shouted Freddie
politely.

Now the Bobbseys' Aunt Sallie Pry was a kind
person and the twins were very fond of her. Her one
drawback was that she was very deaf. This fact often
led to odd and amusing situations. Just now, when
they were rushing to get ready for the trip to Fairy
Lake, a visit from Aunt Sallie, who was not a real
aunt at all, was certainly likely to make it hard for
the Bobbseys. However, they invited her in very
politely and Nan ran to help her take off her hat and
coat.

"Mother isn't home, Aunt Sallie——"

"What—gone to Rome?" said the old lady, cupping
a hand to her ear. "That's a queer place to go this
time of year. Though I dare say it's warm there—
which is more than can be said for Lakeport."

Freddie and Flossie choked back giggles as Aunt
Sallie looked at them. Nan managed to keep a
straight face as she led the old lady into the living-
room.

"I said Mother has gone shopping, Aunt Sallie— shopping," said Nan in her loudest voice. "I think she will be back soon."

"Oh, well, that's good," said the visitor, making herself at home in the most comfortable chair and rubbing her hands together to warm them. "Because I want to talk to her and your father. I have had news —very exciting news—and I want to ask their advice about something."

As she spoke, Aunt Sallie took a letter from her purse and waved it at the interested children.

"Do you see this? It's news—very important news —from my nephew's lawyer. It came all the way from Moosehead. It says——"

Before Aunt Sallie could tell anything more about the contents of the letter, Waggo seized the envelope playfully and scampered out into the hall with it.

"Oh, oh, don't let the dog tear it!" cried the old lady.

To make things worse, Flossie opened the door just then to see if her mother were coming. Out darted Waggo into the snowy street, the letter in his mouth!

CHAPTER VII

AUNT SALLIE'S LEGACY

"OH, oh, don't let him lose it!" cried Aunt Sallie Pry, almost beside herself.

The twins ran in pursuit of Waggo, while the old lady urged them on from the doorway. She waved her cane again and again.

Dinah, coming to see what all the excitement was about, scolded the children roundly for going out without their coats. She promised all sorts of awful punishment which, of course, she never would carry out.

"Yo' come back heah dis very minute!" she insisted.

All this time Waggo darted about, leading them from one snowdrift to another. Sometimes he would stop until they had almost reached him, then would rush off with a wag of his head and an impish gleam in his eye.

Just when they were beginning to despair of ever catching him, Bert solved the problem. He made a flying rugger tackle that almost buried the little dog and himself in a big drift.

"He got him!" cried Freddie, delighted.

Bert came up triumphantly with the pet in his arms. But in the wild scramble Waggo had dropped the letter!

The Bobbsey boy thrust the little dog into Freddie's arms and plunged back into the snowdrift. This time he came up with the letter.

As he waved the envelope over his head, he heard a shout of laughter from the little twins. He turned in time to see Dinah lose her balance and sit down—*hard*—in a deep bank of snow.

"Lawsy me, now how's I ever gwine git up?" moaned the cook, floundering around helplessly. "Somebody's got to give me a hand, dat's sure, lessen I wants to sit here till de snow melts!"

Fairly aching with laughter, the twins managed to tug and push Dinah to her feet.

"Dat Waggo, he'll be de deaf of us all wiv his wild goin's on," she scolded, flipping the corner of her apron at the dog.

The pet slunk off with his tail between his legs, as if he realized quite well how naughty he had been.

"Yo' chilluns go in an' git yo'selves warmed up while I makes yo' some hot cocoa."

"Oh, can it be a party for Aunt Sallie Pry?" begged Flossie.

The tea-party turned out to be fun. The small twins drew up a table in front of the open fire. Flossie found and lighted some candles. Dinah provided the cocoa and some of the batch of cookies she had baked that morning.

"Please tell us about your letter," begged Flossie of Aunt Sallie.

The old lady had put the important envelope back in her handbag and refused to bring it out again.

"I shall wait until your mother gets home," she said firmly.

Presently Bert remarked that Moosehead, where

the letter had come from, was not far from Fairy
Lake. At that the deaf old lady broke in with a sharp:

" 'Fairly bake?' Nonsense, no one could fairly bake
in Lakeport. It's much too cold!"

"I said Fairy Lake, Aunt Sallie," Bert shouted
patiently.

Before they were through with the tea-party
strange packages began to arrive from the stores in
town.

"This one has my snow suit in it. I know from the
shape," said Nan, choosing one of the bulkier parcels.
"I'm going to open it."

She clipped the strings of the package, pushed back
the paper eagerly, then groaned. This was not a new
snow suit, but a fluffy bathroom rug!

"Well, maybe you can wear that," laughed Bert.
"It would be something new, anyway—a bathroom
rug snow suit."

It was nearly dinner-time when Mr. and Mrs.
Bobbsey arrived. Mr. Kape was with them. Each one
came into the living-room laden down with bundles.

"Such a day!" the children's mother was beginning,
when she saw old Mrs. Pry. "Why, hallo!" she said.
"This *is* a pleasant surprise. When did you get here,
Aunt Sallie, and why didn't you let us know you were
coming so we could have sent the car for you?"

"I've had news from my nephew's lawyers," said
Mrs. Pry, brushing the question aside. "Do you
remember John, the one that ran away when he was
a boy to make his fortune?"

"Why, yes, of course. But what about him?"

"Well, he's dead and what's more, he's left me a
legacy."

"Legacy!"

"That's what I said," retorted Aunt Sallie tartly. "And it's the queerest legacy you ever heard of. John Pry might just as well have left me a zoo or an aquarium. Either one of them would have been just about as useful to me as what he did leave."

"What *did* he leave you——"

"Grieve me? Well, no, I can't say it did. You see, I haven't seen John Pry for some twenty years, so why his death should grieve me, I'm sure I don't know."

"I said, what did he *leave* you? The legacy?" said Mrs. Bobbsey, raising her voice.

"Oh, the legacy. Well, you'd never believe it, but what John Pry up and left me was nothing less than an hotel. Did you ever *hear* of anything so ridiculous?"

"What are you going to do with it, Aunt Sallie?" asked Nan.

"That's what I wanted your father's advice about," said the old lady. "I don't know what in the world to do with it."

"I'd keep it," advised Flossie.

"Yes, and run it. Why not?" said Nan, her eyes sparkling.

"I never heard of such nonsense!" replied Aunt Sallie.

"Oh, it would be lots of fun," cried Freddie.

"Where is this hotel?" Mr. Bobbsey wanted to know.

"At a place called Moosehead. Ridiculous name. Here, I have the letter." Mrs. Pry pulled it from her handbag. "It's from John's lawyer and it seems to be entirely legal and all that. Here, read it and tell me what you think of it," she added, thrusting the envelope towards Mr. Bobbsey.

"Well, the hotel seems to belong to you without a doubt," said the children's father, when he had read the document carefully. "The question is, what do you want to do about it?"

"I want to sell it. That's what I came to you about. I want you to help me write a letter to my lawyer," replied the old lady.

"Oh, don't do that, Aunt Sallie, it would be a shame," cried Nan.

"Nonsense! What do I know about running a hotel? And how would I get out to Moosehead all by myself, I'd like to know?" the old lady objected.

"That's the easiest part," argued Bert. "Moosehead is so close to Fairy Lake that it wouldn't be any trouble at all for us to take you there. Would it, Dad?" said the lad, appealing to his father. "We could just drop Aunt Sallie off on the way to the Ice Carnival."

"Drop me off!" sniffed the deaf lady. "And what would I do after I was dropped off, I'd like to know. Just sit there in the middle of an hotel I never saw before, I suppose, and hope that it would run itself."

Flossie giggled at this, but Nan suggested that they might all get together and help Mrs. Pry manage the place.

"I could be chambermaid——"

"And I'd be the cook," giggled Freddie. "I'll get Dinah to show me how."

"I could answer the telephone," offered Flossie. "I *know* I can do that."

"And I could be the receptionist," laughed Bert. "You see, Aunt Sallie, you have all the servants you need already. And all from the Bobbsey family!"

"Well, now," she said, "maybe if——"

It was doubtful whether the old lady could understand all that had been said. But it was plain to the children that she was interested in the suggestion of at least seeing the place. The idea of a trip to Moosehead in the company of the Bobbsey family was a temptation to her.

Meanwhile, there were the fascinating packages to examine. After dinner the twins coaxed their mother to let them see her purchases. Soon they were in the midst of the most delightful confusion of wrapping-paper, tangled cord, snow suits, skates, mittens and scarves that it would be possible to imagine. The youngsters begged to be permitted to try on their new things.

Flossie had a skating-outfit that was as like her dolly's as Mrs. Bobbsey had been able to find. When the little girl, dressed in the flaring skirt and tight little jacket, turned and pirouetted delightedly before the mirror, she looked not unlike a big doll herself.

Nan had a lovely outfit of her own. The thing that delighted her most, however, was a fine new pair of racing-skates which were attached to a pair of very high-laced boots.

"Oh, they're lovely, Mother, and they fit just exactly right," she said, balancing on the knife-sharp edge and clutching at her father for support.

"Whoops!" shouted Freddie suddenly. "Out of my way, everybody!"

He had put on his new skis and came swooping into the room. He stumbled over one of the packages, knocked his sister off balance, and fell with her into the middle of the room.

"Freddie! Freddie! What will you do next?" exclaimed Mrs. Bobbsey.

As the youngsters were picking themselves up, Bert made a discovery. He had opened a package with another snow suit in it. The coat was not very pretty and he wondered why Mrs. Bobbsey had bought it. Then his eye caught a name on the paper.

"Mother, here's a parcel that doesn't belong to us. It says Danny Rugg on it!" he exclaimed.

Mention of the young bully's name sobered the twins instantly. Here was a chance for him to make trouble.

"You must call up Danny at once, Bert," said Mrs. Bobbsey firmly. "Tell him of the mistake and promise to take the suit over to his house first thing in the morning."

"You might know this would happen!" said Bert darkly. "Danny Rugg, of all people!"

Bert came back from the telephone looking madder than ever.

"Danny slammed down the telephone before I could finish speaking," he announced.

"Oh, well, you can take the package over to him in the morning and that will be the end of it," said his mother.

Unfortunately, that was far from being the end of it. About half an hour later the front door-bell rang viciously. When Dinah went to answer it Danny pushed past her rudely and burst into the living-room.

"Where's my suit?" demanded the unpleasant boy. "What have you done with it? I suppose you got it all dirty."

"It's over there on the couch, all tied up the way it was when we got it," said Nan.

Danny eyed the twins' outfits with an ugly scowl.

worser," the old cook grumbled. "Sumpin' ought to be done 'bout dat boy, sure 'nough."

Meanwhile, the bully was forgotten in the excitement of preparations for the trip. Perhaps it was just as well they did not know that Danny had tried to exchange his suit for something more like the one Bert had. He had not been able to do so, because the suit had become wrinkled and a little dirty by being in the snow. This gave the boy one more reason for trying to get even with the Bobbseys.

Aunt Sallie Pry had made up her mind to go to Fairy Lake; or at least as far as Moosehead, where her hotel was located. The children were delighted, of course, for the old lady's legacy sounded very exciting to them and they were looking forward with eagerness to seeing it.

"I'll have to get some new clothes," said Aunt Sallie Pry. "At least a warm coat."

Since Mrs. Bobbsey was so busy with the needs of her family, the twins were asked to help. The next morning found them on their way to a fur shop to buy the needed coat. The deaf old lady was very hard to serve, as she was always mistaking "jargon" for "bargain" and "steal" for "seal" in a very embarrassing way.

The little twins enjoyed these mistakes and chuckled over them happily. The proprietor was an old friend of the Bobbsey children. He had been of great help in choosing their outfits for their wonderful and long-to-be-remembered trip to Eskimo Land. He was not as amused as were the children at Mrs. Pry's queer ways. He was patient and good-natured, however, and in the end persuaded her to buy a sealskin coat.

"It will keep you warm in the coldest climate," he said.

Bert and Nan left the little twins with Aunt Sallie while they went on to the railway station to buy her ticket to Fairy Lake. As they came away from the ticket-office a few minutes later, Nan thought she saw Danny Rugg sneak around a corner of the platform.

"I wonder what he's doing here," she said to her brother.

Nothing more was seen of the unpleasant boy, so they soon forgot about the incident. The next day Nan was to remember it, however, to her sorrow.

The time for leaving arrived. The Bobbseys, Mr. Kape, and Mrs. Pry were gathered on the station platform, waiting excitedly for the train which was to take them to Fairy Lake. Around them was piled their luggage. Mrs. Bobbsey counted the pieces over and over again, determined, so she said, that nothing should be left behind on *this* trip.

It was within a few minutes of train time—Flossie was sure she had heard the whistle of the train in the distance—when something strange happened. A policeman came up to the group and said he would like to have a few words with the young boy there, Bert Bobbsey.

"Why, of course, officer," said the lad's father, surprised but not in the least disturbed. "I'm afraid you will have to be quick about it, though. We expect our train along any minute. What's wrong? Has my son been throwing snowballs through someone's plate-glass window?"

"No, sir. You see it's about a little matter of money." The officer was plainly ill at ease. "I hate to mention it, sir," he added almost apologetically, "but there's been a charge made against your son which it's my duty to investigate."

"Good gracious! You don't mean that Bert has been accused of taking money!" cried Mrs. Bobbsey, outraged.

The little twins were wide-eyed with surprise, and Nan moved closer to Bert as though to protect her twin.

"Well, I wouldn't say quite that, ma'am," the officer said, turning abruptly to Bert. "You bought a ticket here yesterday morning, didn't you, sonny?" he asked.

"Why, yes, I did," replied Bert. "My sister was with me. We bought a ticket to Fairy Lake for Mrs. Pry here."

"Can you tell me where you got the money?" asked the officer, eyeing Bert closely.

"Why, from Aunt Sallie—Mrs. Pry, of course," replied the boy.

"You can prove that, I suppose?"

Here Aunt Sallie, who had been listening intently, her sharp eyes on both the policeman and Bert, interrupted.

"He doesn't have to prove anything, officer. I'm Mrs. Pry and I gave him the money to buy the ticket. Now what more do you want?"

Before the man could answer, Flossie called out shrilly, "Here comes Danny Rugg with his father and mother. I wonder if he's going to Fairy Lake on our train."

At the same moment the bully noticed the Bobbsey family group. He tried to dodge out of sight, but was too late.

"Hi there, you!" called the policeman. "Yes, you!"

as Danny hesitated. "Come over here a minute. I've something to say to you."

The bully approached reluctantly, followed by his mother and father.

"This is the lad who made the charge against you," the officer told Bert. "He said you stole the money for the ticket you bought yesterday. How about it, my lad?" he added, as Danny fidgeted uneasily, his eyes fixed on the ground. "Have you anything more to say? Be quick about it now," he added, "for, unless I'm very much mistaken, here comes your train. Quick now! Do you take back the charge?"

As people surged forward, Danny still hesitated. He shot a furious glance at Bert, but the presence of his mother and father made him change his mind about what he had been going to say. He shifted from one foot to the other and mumbled:

"Maybe I made a mistake. I don't know."

But the officer persisted. He had only a moment, but he meant to get the matter straight.

"You drop the charge then, do you?" he demanded.

Most of the passengers already had boarded the train. The guard was waving his hand and shouting "All aboard!" Danny had only a moment to make up his mind.

"Sure, I drop the charge. Forget it, will you?" he said and brushed past the Bobbsey group so rudely that he almost knocked Aunt Sallie down!

Mr. and Mrs. Rugg were shocked at their son's actions. They apologized for Danny, at the same time helping the sputtering old lady into the train. Mrs. Pry was more annoyed than she was hurt.

"That dreadful boy!" she fumed. "Terrible things

are going to happen to him if something isn't done
about him."

They got her settled at last, however, and the
Bobbseys were free to look about them. The coach
was full of people who, like themselves, were bound
for Moosehead, which was the nearest railway
station to Fairy Lake. They were a jolly lot, off for
a holiday.

Mr. Kape knew the ones who were going to per-
form at the Ice Carnival, so he introduced them to
the Bobbsey family. The twins found themselves the
centre of a merry group. They recognized one famous
name after another. Freddie and Flossie grew so
excited their eyes nearly popped from their heads.

"And this is Eric Townsend," said Mr. Kape.
"He'll keep you laughing at his jokes."

The children had seen this actor on the movies and
had often laughed at his clowning. He was also an
expert skier. Now to see him in person was indeed a
treat. It was strange to find that he was just like anyone else!

"Oh, call me Eric the Red," he said when Nan
spoke to him as Mr. Townsend. "Everyone does."

Because of his wavy, blond, reddish hair and his
generally sandy complexion, the actor was called
"Eric the Red" by his friends. It was not long before
others did so, and pretty soon the twins were using
the nicknames as freely as the rest.

The man was great fun. He was one of those
comical people who can make a joke out of nothing,
just by the way he tells it. Soon everybody in the
coach was laughing at the things he said and saying
funny things to one another back and forth across
the aisles.

"Look back there," said Nan to Bert after a while. "Look at Danny's face."

The only one who was not enjoying himself seemed to be Danny Rugg. The boy had been severely scolded by his parents and now sat by himself in the rear of the coach. He divided his time between frowning at the landscape and scowling at the twins. He paid no attention to Eric the Red.

The Bobbseys were having too good a time to bother with the bully. Even Aunt Sallie Pry rocked with laughter as the clown ambled up the aisle, making funny remarks about everyone and pretending to discover what was wrong with each one of them in turn.

"The trouble with this little girl," said Eric the Red, stopping beside Flossie, "is that she thinks she's just an ordinary little girl. Really she's a fairy princess from—let's see—Titania Land. Some day her fairy godmother will come along and wave a wand and—presto!—back she'll be on her throne in the Palace of Make-Believe. All the rest of us will be her willing servants."

"Oh, do you really think so?" cried Flossie, clapping her hands.

"It will happen almost any day now," said Eric the Red gravely.

CHAPTER IX

THE CLOWN HELPS

FLOSSIE was delighted to hear she might become a fairy princess. She took her new friend's words so seriously that she went around all the rest of the day with such a queenly air that others in the train had to laugh at her.

"I guess I'll have to change your name from Fat Fairy to Fairy Princess," laughed her daddy. From that time on the little girl and Eric the Red were fast friends. It was an hour or two after her meeting with the famous actor that Flossie suddenly had her great idea. The other children saw her draw the clown aside and whisper to him earnestly.

For some time this secret conversation continued. When the two finally rejoined the group of skiers and skaters, they seemed to have come to a complete agreement on something of importance.

"Quiet, please," said Eric the Red, raising his hand for silence. "My little friend here has made an interesting suggestion and I have promised to pass it along to you."

The voices and laughter died off to a murmur while the actors looked curiously at Flossie and Eric the Red.

"It seems our good friend here, Aunt Sallie Pry," continued Eric, with an elaborate bow in the old lady's direction, "has inherited an hotel at Moosehead. Not many people are there. It is Flossie's idea that we give the place a try. What do you say, troopers? Shall we do it? All in favour say 'aye'."

Now show people are probably the most generous-hearted folk in the world, as everyone knows who has had anything to do with them. So now, looking at Flossie's eager little face, they shouted "aye" with the heartiest good will.

The little girl was delighted, of course, as were her brothers and sister. Only Aunt Sallie did not seem as pleased as they thought she should. Mrs. Pry was alarmed at the idea of entertaining all these strange people at an hotel she had never seen. But she thanked Flossie just the same for her good intentions. She said the little girl was very thoughtful.

At noon that day in the dining-car Nan had a delightful time. She was introduced to pretty, twelve-year-old Shirley Swift, and sat down to eat with her. The young skating star was well known. Already she had been in two or three motion pictures. Shirley was one of Nan's great favourites on the screen and it was a tremendous thrill to be with her.

"I'm so glad to meet you," the young actress said to Nan. "I've been a little lonely. You probably think screen children have everything on earth. But we don't have much chance to play with other children."

The waiter had just brought the soup and the two girls were having a very good time, when Danny Rugg passed by on his way to his own table. At once he became jealous of Nan's good fortune. Bad boy that he was, he instantly wanted to do something to embarrass her.

As Nan raised a spoonful of soup to her mouth, the

unpleasant boy lurched against her. The hot liquid went flying! Some of it splashed on the table-cloth, some on Shirley's pretty dress.

Then all was confusion and excitement. Poor Nan apologized for her clumsiness, saying over and over again how sorry she was. Danny Rugg was passing on with a self-satisfied grin on his face when he felt himself suddenly seized from behind. His hands were held behind his back so that he was helpless to move. He looked up, scowling, into the face of Eric the Red.

"Hey, let go, will you? You're hurting me!" he yelled.

"It's no more than you deserve, you mean boy!" said the clown, scowling back at the captive. "I saw what you did, pushing against Nan on purpose. Say you're sorry, quick, before I throw you out of the window!"

Of course he never would have done such a thing, but Eric looked ferocious enough to scare the bully. Danny muttered something about being sorry and was released so suddenly that he staggered and almost fell in the aisle.

After lunch Bert overheard a conversation between his father and Mr. Kape which set him wondering a little about Aunt Sallie Pry's inheritance. Feeling lazy after his hearty lunch, the boy had stretched out in a corner of the seat to read. He heard Mr. Kape say:

"I don't know whether that was such a good idea of Flossie's, asking Eric the Red and all the other entertainers to stay at the Central Hotel. I'm afraid they may be a little disappointed with the place."

"What makes you think so?" asked Mr. Bobbsey. "Isn't the hotel in good shape?"

"Well, it's a trifle run-down and shabby. The service isn't all that could be desired." Mr. Kape seemed to hesitate, then continued unwillingly, "If the truth must be told, I'm afraid the former owner of the Central neglected it sadly in the past few years. People just don't go there any more."

"H'm, that's too bad. I'm afraid Aunt Sallie will be very much disappointed. We persuaded her to make this trip, you know," said the twins' father. After a minute of silence Mr. Bobbsey added, "Do you think there is any chance of selling the Central? It should be worth something to a man who would know how to run it."

"The problem would be to find a buyer who had money enough to fix up the place," Mr. Kape replied. "Such buyers don't grow on bushes, you know. In the meantime, I think Eric and the others would be much better off at my brother's place, the Windham. That's a really up-and-coming hotel; good service, good meals, pleasant location, everything."

"Well, we'll have to think it over." Bert could tell by his father's voice that he was worried. "Meanwhile, if you hear of a possible buyer please let me know. After what you have told me, it looks as if Aunt Sallie's best chance would be to try to sell the place."

At this point Mr. Bobbsey and his friend went off. Bert was left to think over what he had heard. Was Mrs. Pry to be disappointed, after all, just when she was becoming interested in her strange inheritance? Bert resolved to try to find some way to help the old lady.

Turning to look out of the window again the boy was surprised to find that snow was beginning to fall.

It looked, indeed, as if they were running into some very bad weather. The skies were overcast and the wind was rising.

The train rumbled on for some time at good speed, but gradually the storm began to have its effect. It became more and more difficult for the driver to see ahead. Suddenly with a shrill scream of the whistle and a jolt that jarred all the passengers in their seats, the express came to a complete stop.

"We've hit something!" cried Aunt Sallie Pry excitedly.

At once the coach in which the Bobbseys and their new friends were riding was filled with confusion. Questions were asked which no one bothered to answer. People rushed up and down the aisles, demanding to speak with the guard.

Mr. Bobbsey decided to go outside and see for himself what had happened. Perhaps he could help if there had been an accident. Nan and Bert followed their father after hustling into warm clothing. Ducking their heads against the keen wind, they slid and stumbled down the steps and out into the snow.

They could see their father ahead of them, half-hidden by the heavily falling flakes, in conversation with one of the guards. As they came closer they heard the guard say:

"We ran through one of the switch signals, sir. Lucky we were going slow when we bumped into the goods train ahead of us, or the passengers would have got something worse than a shaking up."

Bert was about to speak when he saw a sly figure slip out of the goods train and dart away across the tracks.

"That's Beany Ferris!" he cried. "The man who probably robbed the Kapes' home!"

Without giving himself time to consider what he was doing, or what might be the result of his rash action, the boy rushed across the tracks after the man.

CHAPTER X

AN ADVENTURE

NOW of course Nan never should have followed her twin. It was a foolish thing to do. She should have warned her father that Bert had run off after the man called Beany. Instead, she hurried away herself.

"Bert! Bert!" she called.

After she had gone some distance across the tracks and both Bert and the train were hidden from her by the falling snow, Nan began to feel afraid.

"Bert, where are you?" she called again, this time with fright in her voice.

There was no answer, so the girl paused for a moment, wondering whether to go on or return to the train. She decided to struggle on, knowing that her twin could not be very far away and feeling sure that each step would bring her to him.

"Come back, Bert!" she screamed as loudly as she could.

Meanwhile, Mr. Bobbsey, thinking that the twins had boarded the train ahead of him, got into another coach. There he saw a man from Lakeport he knew and stopped to talk with him.

The whistle blew, the train jolted, started, jolted again and then started. Cautiously it felt its way backwards towards the junction where it had passed the signal light.

Everyone aboard was relieved that the damage had been so slight. Eric the Red did some of his clowning stunts to cheer up those who had been nervous. Freddie and Flossie tried to explain something about the carnival to deaf Aunt Sallie Pry.

"I guess it's no use," said the little girl finally to her twin. "We'll let Bert and Nan do it."

Alas, no one realized that Bert and Nan were not aboard the train!

Meanwhile, the Bobbsey boy, not knowing that the train had left without him, had nearly caught up with Beany Ferris. As the fellow stopped to light a cigarette, Bert caught the gleam of the match and ploughed forward eagerly. The man turned at his approach and scowled, flinging the burnt match into the snow.

"What do you want?" he demanded roughly.

"You're Beany Ferris, aren't you?" Bert asked hurriedly.

"So what?" demanded the fellow, lighting another match with shaky fingers. "Is it anything to you? Who's that?" he added sharply, pointing past Bert into the gloom.

"It's Nan, Bert—Nan," said a tired girl's voice. "I've been looking for you. I thought I'd never find you."

Bert put out his hand to his sister and she grasped it thankfully.

"Oh, Bert, I'm so glad. I was getting scared," she faltered.

The red-haired man had seemed relieved to find that the newcomer was only a girl—a rather frightened one at that. Now, however, suspicion

flared anew in the deep-set eyes under bushy brows.
He demanded gruffly:

"What do you kids want, anyway? Why did you
follow me here?"

Nan gripped her brother's arm and whispered, "I
don't like him, Bert. Let's go back!"

The boy took no notice of his sister. Instead, he
took a step towards the red-haired man and looked
at him steadily.

"You are Beany Ferris," he charged. "And you're
wanted by the police back at Lakeport."

"Yeah? So what?" sneered the man. "You've got
the police with you, I suppose. Have you?" he added,
his voice suddenly rough, his eyes hard.

"No, I haven't," said Bert. "But I know you were
sneaking around the Kapes' house on the day of the
fire. I saw you there."

"So what?" demanded the man again.

"So you went back afterwards and tried to steal
whatever it was you couldn't get away with on the day
of the fire," said Bert, ignoring Nan's frantic tug at
the boy's coatsleeve. "For all I know," he added,
struck by a sudden thought, "you may have set the
house afire on purpose."

The fellow seemed to have satisfied himself that the
children were really alone. As he had nothing to fear
from them, he looked at the twins with a sneering smile
and flicked the half-smoked cigarette into the snow.

"You can think what you like," he told them.
"You're two crazy kids and it don't make no difference
to me if you call me Captain Kidd or some other
pirate. But whoever you are you'd better get out of
these here woods if you don't want to be snowed under
a foot deep. So long. I'll be seeing you—maybe!"

With a mocking wave of the hand, the fellow turned and disappeared into the gathering gloom.

"We'd better be g-getting back to the t-train," said Nan, her teeth chattering with cold. "Oh, Bert, I'm afraid of that awful man!"

"He's Beany Ferris, all right," said the boy excitedly as he and his sister began to battle their way towards the railway tracks. "The police chief at home let me see a picture of him, and this is the man. I couldn't be mistaken. I wonder what he's doing out here?"

Nan was too tired and cold to care much just then about Beany Ferris. She was beginning to realize that it was a long time since they had left the halted train. Their parents would be worried about them, she was sure.

The snow had deepened. In places it almost covered up the trail they had made. The marks still were to be seen enough, though, so that they could be followed. By keeping faithfully to them and ploughing ahead steadily, brother and sister finally reached the tracks.

"Bert!" cried Nan suddenly. "The train! It's gone!"

For a moment the youngsters could not believe their eyes. They stared at the empty rails as if, just by looking hard enough, they could wish the familiar train back again.

"Maybe it—it isn't far away," said Bert hopefully.

But it was no use. As far as they could see the track stretched ahead, bleak and empty. Only the goods train, which their own engine had rammed, remained on the siding, the tops of its trucks blanketed in deep, soft snow.

"Bert, they've gone off and left us!" cried Nan.

"Mother and Dad must have thought we were aboard," said Bert, shading his eyes to stare up the empty track. "Gee, what shall we do now?"

"I—I don't know," replied Nan, shivering as the wind bit through her heavy coat. "If we stand around like this we'll freeze to death. Don't you suppose there's some place near here where we can go to get warm?"

"There must be," said Bert, who felt he should be manly and protect his sister. He peered about him in an effort to pierce the curtain of heavily falling snow. "Where there's a goods siding and a lot of switches there's bound to be a signal-box. Let's look."

Pulling their coats closer about them and slapping themselves to keep warm, the children trudged along the snowy track. As they had to keep their heads down against the wind, they did not see the signal-box until they were almost upon it. The twins never before had seen half so welcome a sight!

"There's a light," said Bert. "We're all right now."

They clasped hands and began to run, floundering and slipping, towards the light which was high up. At last they reached the building. After feeling about the base of it for a time, the twins found a door. They pushed this open and let themselves in.

How good the place felt and how good something smelled! It was warm and someone overhead was cooking. The odour of toast floated down temptingly to the hungry children.

Nan was sniffing the air longingly when something soft and furry rubbed against her ankle. She picked up the little welcoming ball of fur and held it against her cold cheek, cuddling it fondly.

"Look, Bert, what a darling kitten! Black from top to toe, not a spot of white anywhere. I'd like to take it away with me."

"You'd much better take anything else I've got, young lady. I wouldn't give up that kitten for any amount of money. No, sir, she's a trick cat," said a pleasant voice.

The twins turned around to find a tall, lanky person regarding them curiously but kindly. This was the man in charge of the signal-box. The children told him their story and found he was ready to help them out of their difficulties.

First he took them into a comfortable, well-lighted little office behind the signal room. There he gave them cocoa, toast, and some sandwiches from his lunch-box. Then he told them what he could do for them. All this while he was making the black kitten do tricks he had taught it.

"There's a train due through here in about twenty minutes," he explained. "That cuts across country and will reach Glover Junction a few minutes before your express comes through. Once at that station all you have to do is go across the tracks and get aboard your own train.

"Meanwhile, I'll phone on ahead to the station nearest to the express. I'll tell the ticket-collector there to give your parents a message saying you are safe and will see them soon."

Nan and Bert thought the man was very kind to take so much trouble for them. They told him so, but he only laughed and said he was very glad to be of service.

Their new friend was as good as his word. When the cross-country train arrived he put the twins aboard personally. The last they saw of him was his big, ungainly figure, bundled up to the chin in a heavy coat, standing on the rough platform at the siding.

"He's a darling," decided Nan, "and so is his cat."

It was an anxious ride for the twins. They were worried for fear the train they were on would fail to reach the junction ahead of the express. Anything might happen, they knew, in such a bad storm. A delay of no more than five minutes might make all the difference between meeting the express and missing it.

"What shall we do if we should miss it?" said Nan over and over again, getting more worried every minute.

CHAPTER XI

A COLD WELCOME

"OH, everything will be all right," Bert tried to cheer his sister, but he wondered himself if it would be. He was mighty glad when he heard a voice cry out:

"Glover Junction next! All out for Glover Junction!"

The place proved to be a strange and frightening one. There were so many tracks that the twins did not know which might be the one they wanted. It seemed hopeless to try to find the right one.

"Nobody seems to know," sighed Bert after he had asked several people.

Finally they reached the right place just in the nick of time. A huge path of light bit through the snowy mist and the express roared into the junction!

Mr. and Mrs. Bobbsey were waiting on the platform of the train to greet the runaways. Mrs. Bobbsey's face was white with strain and when she tried to smile at the twins, tears stood in her eyes.

"I've been so worried," she said. "Darlings, how could you have done such a thing! We were frightened to death!"

Mr. Bobbsey was a little stern at first and tried to scold the children, but he was so glad to have them back that the scolding was a very gentle one.

Bert said he was very sorry. "It all happened because I chased Beany Ferris," he explained.

This was the first time that anyone but Nan had heard about Beany Ferris. The little twins who had been regarding their brother and sister with big eyes, demanded to know all about the red-haired man. Mr. Kape listened with especial attention as the boy told his story. He promised to send word to the police of the little town towards which Beany had fled.

"I'll warn them that he's in their neighbourhood," Mr. Kape said. "Bert, even if you did give everyone a scare, you did a good deed."

Although Moosehead was the next stop, the little twins could not keep their eyes open another moment. It had been a long day for them. They curled up in the big seats and soon were fast asleep.

Nan and Bert were tired, too, but they were excited as well, now that the end of the journey was in sight. They went to sit beside Aunt Sallie Pry, who seemed very nervous.

"I never should have come way up here on such a wild-goose chase," she said, as the girl slipped into the seat beside her. "An hotel I've never seen, indeed! Suppose the food is bad or the roof leaks. What'll I do then?"

"Fix the roof, I suppose," said Nan sleepily.

Aunt Sallie pounced on her.

"Fix! I should say it is a fix! And no way to get out of it, either, that I can see."

Nan was too tired to argue with the old lady. She tried to say something comforting but broke off in the middle of it and fell into a rather worried silence. Like Bert, she had overheard her parents talking of the hotel and had gathered that the place was run-down and shabby.

"Suppose it turns out to be an awful place!" she thought anxiously. "Suppose the place is cold, the beds hard, the food poor!"

What possible excuse could they make to Eric the Red and his merry troupe for asking them to go there? To make matters worse Freddie, not to be outdone by his little sister, had invited several musicians on the train to make the Central their headquarters, too!

"Anyway," she shouted at Aunt Sallie, "you're going with us to the Windham tonight and you can get a good rest."

Nan must have dropped asleep with this thought. At any rate, the next thing she knew her mother was shaking her gently and Bert was saying in a very loud voice:

"Wake up, sleepyhead! We're pulling into the station."

It was even harder to rouse the little twins. They had been deep into dreamland and staggered about in the aisle while Mrs. Bobbsey and Aunt Sallie coaxed them into their coats and hats.

It seemed to the twins that everybody on the train had got off at Moosehead. The crowds, the excitement and the sparkling cold air shook everyone wide awake.

"There's Mrs. Kape," cried Bert, and led the others to the waiting woman.

Mrs. Kape's husband kissed her and there was a lot of handshaking. Then the woman said that she was sorry but she had some unpleasant news for the Bobbseys.

"Unfortunately I couldn't get any accommodation

for you at the Windham," she said. "But I telephoned the Central and they are holding rooms for you. I hope you don't mind."

The Bobbseys and Aunt Sallie Pry looked at one another, not knowing how to answer. Finally the children's mother said:

"Maybe it will work out better that way. You see Mrs. Pry is the new owner of the Central and we can be right there to help her attend to things."

"I have a big car in which to take you," said Mrs. Kape. "I guess we all can squeeze into it."

Wondering what would happen at the hotel, the Bobbseys followed her to the car. As they all crowded in they had to laugh and so forgot their worries for the time being. Mr. Bobbsey said jokingly:

"Instead of two pairs of twins I'll have two pairs of sardines by the time we reach the Central!"

Nobody really minded the crowding, however. The fact that they had actually reached the region of Fairy Lake and were about to see Aunt Sallie's inheritance made up for everything else.

As they slithered and slid along the snowy road, Freddie pressed his little nose against the glass. He pointed at every group of lights they passed, demanding to know:

"Is that the Central over there?"

They reached it at last. Mrs. Kape turned in through a pair of sagging gates. The road led upwards to a building darkly outlined against the sky. There were lights in it but they were so dim that it was impossible to tell from the outside what the place was like.

"I hope it's more cheerful inside," Nan whispered to Bert.

As they reached the porch, no one came out to help them with their cases. By the aid of one light coming through a dirty globe over the door they got out of the car.

"H'm, fine service, I must say," Aunt Sallie muttered. "I'll tell those people a thing or two when we get inside!"

Mr. Bobbsey pushed open the door impatiently and his family trooped in. The lobby was badly lighted and smelled as if it had not been aired properly nor cleaned for months.

A rumpled, untidy-looking night porter jumped up as they entered and eyed them sullenly. From his appearance they judged that he had been taking a comfortable nap behind the counter when they arrived. It was evident that he did not like being disturbed.

"You have rooms for us," said the twins' father. "I am Mr. Bobbsey and this," drawing Aunt Sallie forward, "is Mrs. Pry, the new owner of the Central."

The porter did not answer. He just looked at Aunt Sallie as if to say that new owners meant nothing to him. He wasn't interested in the least!

"You have our reservations, I suppose," said Mr. Bobbsey, annoyed.

The porter thumbed over his book. He admitted grudgingly that he had reserved rooms for the party. He took several keys from a rack and motioned to a sleepy-eyed bell-boy.

"Go and tell Mr. and Mrs. Kape we have reservations," Mr. Bobbsey told Bert. "They need not wait any longer."

When the lad returned, the Bobbsey party followed

the bell-boy into a creaking lift. They were taken to the second floor.

"I don't like this place," whimpered Flossie snuggling her hand into Nan's. "It's not nice."

Nan put a finger to her lips. "Don't let Aunt Sallie hear you," she warned.

The rooms on the second floor were even less attractive than the lobby. They were shabby and cold, with dim lighting and lumpy beds. Aunt Sallie sank down into one of the old chairs and burst into tears. Nan and Mrs. Bobbsey tried to comfort the poor lady.

"The place will look much better by daylight," they said. "Try not to worry."

Suddenly there was the sound of a great commotion in the downstairs lobby. Nan exchanged a look with her brother.

"There's Eric the Red and his troupe," she said.

When the older twins reached the lower floor they found Eric the Red engaged in words with the surly night porter. The other professional skaters, skiers, and musicians for the Ice Carnival were talking loudly, too.

"That's a fine way to run an hotel," Eric was saying. "I merely ask you for rooms and you tell me you don't want people here who make any noise."

"I asked you to be quiet so other guests could sleep," the porter defended himself.

"You might have asked us politely," replied Eric the Red. "Anyway, that has nothing to do with giving us rooms."

"He's too lazy to bother," spoke up the musician who played the saxophone.

Actually this was the truth. The porter did not want to bother with so many people. He looked guilty.

"Well, I—uh—I——" he began.

Eric already had picked up his cases and was striding towards the door. "Let's get out of here," he said to his friends. "We'll go over to the Windham. That's a real hotel."

The actor was half-way to the door when he looked up and saw Nan and Bert on the stairs. He turned red and stammered apologetically:

"Sorry, but I guess we'll have to go somewhere else. Our friend here," with a jerk of his thumb towards the porter, "doesn't seem to want us. We make too much noise."

"Well, *we* want you," said Nan with spirit, running up to the man. "And I guess that's what counts. Aunt Sallie Pry owns this hotel and what she says goes! She wouldn't turn you away."

Meanwhile, Bert had approached the desk. He tried to make his expression as stern as possible as he spoke to the sullen porter.

"These people are friends of ours. I suppose you have enough rooms for them all, haven't you?" he demanded.

"Depends on how many they want," said the man. Then he added grudgingly, "We could give them the whole third floor, I suppose."

"That will be lovely," said Nan brightly. "They can have the whole place to themselves."

Eric the Red and his troupe as well as the musicians looked as if they thought this would be anything but "lovely". They said nothing more, however, about leaving. They were given keys and departed for the third floor.

"This is some lift," the twins heard Eric say. "Nice musical squeak," he laughed. "You'd better put it in your band, Tommy!"

The Bobbsey children looked at each other, not knowing whether to be happy or sad.

"I'm sure they wouldn't have stayed here at all if they hadn't promised us beforehand," Nan said mournfully. "This *is* an awful place, isn't it, Bert?"

"Pretty awful," agreed Bert glumly. "I guess Aunt Sallie will have to sell it after all."

"I wonder if anybody would buy it," added his sister, as the twins climbed the stairs.

CHAPTER XII

FLOSSIE MEETS A KING

LUMPY beds or not, the twins were so tired that they slept soundly that night. In the morning they were inclined to take a much more cheerful view of Aunt Sallie Pry's inheritance. Nothing, they reasoned, could be so bad as the Central had seemed to them the night before.

They had not been up very long, however, before they discovered that it could be just as bad—if not worse! The lobby looked even more dreary by daylight than it had the night before.

In the dining-room where the Bobbsey family gathered hungrily they were served half-cooked cereal. With it was thin milk and toast that looked as if it had been burned and scraped before the butter had been put on.

"I wonder if they think we can eat this," said Mrs. Bobbsey, looking in disgust at the unappetizing food on her plate.

"Right after breakfast I mean to have an interview with the manager of this hotel," said Aunt Sallie firmly. "I'd like to see what kind of a man would run a place the way this one is being run. And afterwards," she turned with a grim expression to Mr. Bobbsey, "I want to see my nephew's lawyer. I'm going to sell this hotel just as soon as I can get a buyer for it!"

When the twins left the breakfast table they were still hungry. They thought longingly of Dinah's scrambled eggs and puffy, golden muffins.

"If we stay here much longer, we'll starve to death!" Flossie predicted darkly, as Nan buttoned her into her snug playsuit.

The landscape outside the hotel was as beautiful and inviting as the hotel itself was cold and cheerless. One glance at the rolling hills and the sunlit mountains in the distance was enough to raise the twins' spirits.

Shouting with glee, Flossie and Freddie plunged into a snowdrift. Just then Eric the Red came around the corner of the hotel, his arms full of snowballs.

"Aha, so you want a fight," he cried, on discovering the children. "Well, I'll have you know I'm a born warrior. Nothing delights me more than a good, stiff battle against odds. I'll fight all four of you and I bet I'll beat you without half trying. Up with your defences, now. I'll give you five minutes to get your fort built!"

With a joyful whoop the children accepted the challenge. Working busily, shouting and laughing, they piled up the snow for their fort. Then they packed it solidly along the top. Down on his knees Freddie made snowballs and piled them in a neat mound at the base of the white fort.

"Here, here, we can't have all this noise!" said a fussy voice suddenly. "You will have to stop at once! At once, do you hear me?"

Bert straightened up slowly and dusted the snow

from his mittens. The owner of the stern voice he recognized as the manager of the Central Hotel.

"We're not doing any harm," the boy said. "We——"

Then he stopped looking at this man, to stare beyond him at a boy who had just come down the steps. The boy was Danny Rugg!

"How did *you* get here?" demanded Bert, frowning at the other's self-satisfied grin. "I thought you and your family were going to the Hotel Windham."

"Oh, it was full, so we came here," said Danny carelessly. "It's a stuffy place, too," he added with a glance at the manager. "My dad says it's the worst one he was ever in. He's going to make them take us in at the Windham. He won't stay here another night."

The manager frowned. Then he warned the twins again about making so much noise and went off into the hotel, slamming the door after him.

"He's mean and this *is* an awful place," said Flossie.

The twins waved to Eric the Red and wandered off sadly. Finding Danny at the Central was the last straw, they told themselves.

This mood did not last long, however. The holiday spirit was abroad in Moosehead. It brought out throngs of gaily dressed people all heading in one direction—Fairy Lake. Groups carrying skis and skates passed the children. Laughter and gaiety filled the air.

Suddenly a member of one of these merry groups stopped and waved to Nan. She recognized her new friend, pretty Shirley Swift, and waved back eagerly.

"What are you doing tonight?" called the skater.

"We don't know yet," Nan shouted back.

"We're going on a sleigh ride. Like to come along?" Shirley invited.

"Love to," returned Nan. "I'll find out if we may go."

"All right. I'll see you later. I'm off now to practise for the carnival," said Shirley.

· She waved again and was swept away by her companions. Nan looked after the girl a little enviously.

"I wish I could skate one-tenth as well as she does," the Bobbsey twin sighed.

The children wanted to go to Fairy Lake but their father had told them to wait until he should return from the lawyer's with Aunt Sallie Pry. Then he would go with them. Luckily he returned soon and the five of them set out in the best of spirits for the scene of the coming carnival.

"Goody, goody," said Flossie happily, getting as close to her father as she could.

Mr. Kape had given them very clear directions as to the shortest way. He had promised to meet them at Fairy Lake where he would be practising for his part in the winter show. As they reached the spot Nan cried out:

"Oh, it's wonderful!"

The lake was very beautiful. It lay in a valley surrounded on three sides by snow-covered mountains. Now the morning sun made it glisten like one big jewel. It was already well dotted with skaters and the children paused on the crest of the hill to watch the graceful glides and jumps of the more gifted performers.

"There's Mr. Kape!" called out Bert. "Gee, watch him spin on one foot!"

"Oh, look," said Nan, "he's going to skate with Shirley."

Sure enough, the two began a dance which the twins declared was the most beautiful one they had ever seen. It was hard to tear themselves away from this fascinating sight, but they wanted to see other things, so they went on until they came to the first of the ski jumps.

This was a comparatively easy jump, used by the skiers to "warm up" for their more difficult feats. They paused to watch for a few moments and were about to move on when a shout stopped them.

"Hallo!" called Eric the Red.

He swooped towards them on a beautiful pair of skis, pulling up so close to the little twins that Flossie stepped back and clutched at her father's hand. Freddie stood his ground, though, as a brave little boy should.

"Golly, that's a swell pair of skis, Eric the Red," he said, his eyes sparkling.

"How would you like to use them?" teased the clown, capering in the snow.

"I couldn't. They go too fast," said Freddie. "But I wish I could."

Quick as a thought, Eric caught up the little boy, swinging him on to his shoulders.

"Now hold on to my head," he ordered, laughing, "and away we go over the ski jump. Ready?"

Freddie had just time to gasp out, "Golly, sure I am!" when they were off.

Down the steep incline to the jump, then a short distance on the level and then a sudden take-off into space, flying the way a bird does. Down, down with the wind in their faces and the ground rushing to meet them. Then another long glide, a dizzying swoop as they circled at the end of the course and— it was over!

"I want to go again!" shouted Freddie, as Eric the Red struggled up the incline to rejoin the Bobbseys. "It's the best fun I ever had. Please take me again," begged the little boy.

"No, it's my turn next," put in Flossie. "You can't have all the fun just because you're a boy."

Laughing, Eric swung the little girl on to his shoulders as he had Freddie.

"Hold on," he cried. "Here we go!"

"Careful, Fat Fairy," warned Mr. Bobbsey.

Off they went, with Flossie clinging to Eric's hair and shrieking joyfully. All went well until they nearly reached the bottom. To the consternation of the onlookers, a figure ran from the sidelines and stepped directly in the path of Eric the Red!

"It's Danny!" shrieked Nan, who recognized the boy's snow suit.

Eric tried to dodge, but tripped and fell. Flossie, thrown from her perch on his shoulders, flew headlong through the air!

Everyone rushed to the help of the little girl, where she lay shaken and stunned on the ground—everyone, that is, except Danny Rugg, who had been responsible for the accident.

The first to reach Flossie was a tall, handsome young man whom the twins had never seen before. He lifted the little girl carefully and brushed the snow from her bruised cheek. She opened her eyes, smiled faintly, and patted the smiling stranger's face.

"Who are you?" she asked weakly.

As though to answer her question, a shout went up

from the sidelines of, "Hurray for the King! Long live the King!"

"Are you a king?" asked Flossie, forgetting her hurts and fright.

"King of the Ice Carnival," smiled the handsome young man.

He stood the child on her feet gently just as the Bobbseys came running up.

"Oh, Flossie, are you hurt?" cried Nan, dropping to her knees beside her little sister.

"A little. But it doesn't matter, Nan," said her small sister, staring up in awe and admiration at her new friend, " 'cause I was rescued by a king!"

Everybody laughed at this, especially the Bobbseys. They were so relieved to find that the little twin was not badly hurt that nothing else mattered.

When the King of the Carnival heard who the Bobbseys were, he was very much interested. He said he had never met two sets of twins before and added laughingly:

"I shall have you made members of my court. Every king has princes and princesses around him, you know."

Through the King, whose real name was Victor Comstock, they learned that the Queen of the Carnival was about to be chosen. At once the children wanted to go and watch the end of this exciting contest.

In the confusion everyone had forgotten about poor Eric the Red, who had been pretty badly shaken by his fall. Now he rejoined them, brushing snow from his clothes and vowing punishment on Danny Rugg.

"He tripped me on purpose," the skier declared. "When I catch that boy I'll do more than tie him in knots."

"What will you do?" asked Freddie with interest.

"I'll twist him into a letter X!" said the ski jumper.

When they reached the place where the Queen of the Carnival was being chosen, Bert drew Nan's attention to a pretty girl seated on a bobsled. Photographers were all about her, busy taking pictures.

"I'll bet that's the Queen," said the lad.

In his eagerness to see better the boy drew Nan to one side of a group who were watching the fun. As he did so a camera clicked and one of the photographers hailed him.

"Say, you youngsters aren't supposed to be in this!" he said.

Nan and Bert looked around and saw that the little twins had followed them. All four of the Bobbsey twins had been included in the photographer's picture of the pretty girl!

The children said they were very sorry; that of course they hadn't meant to get in the way. The King, coming towards them just then, smoothed things over for them. He said that it didn't matter in the least, since he proposed to have both sets of twins as members of his court.

Although the children thought their new friend was only joking, they were very much flattered by his attention just the same. Once when they were talking with the King they caught sight of Danny Rugg's scowling face on the outskirts of the crowd. They knew the lad was jealous because they had made the acquaintance of such an important person.

On the way back to the hotel they paused again to watch the skaters. Of them all they were sure Shirley Swift was the best.

The pretty young star waved to Nan. She glided

up to the margin of the lake and pirouetted on the very tips of her skates, smiling at them.

"The sleigh ride has been put off till tomorrow afternoon," said Shirley, "but I hope all of you can come then. Can you?"

Mr. Bobbsey was appealed to and very willingly gave his consent.

"Good!" said Shirley. "See you then!" and sped off, bits of ice flying from her skates.

CHAPTER XIII

MORE MISCHIEF

SO passed the first day at Fairy Lake for the Bobbsey twins. They were so tired that night that they scarcely noticed how poor the dinner was. And the beds at the Central might have been the softest in the world for all they knew or cared. They went to sleep as soon as their heads touched the pillows and did not awaken until their mother came to call them.

"I have something interesting to show you, so hurry downstairs to breakfast," she said mysteriously.

When the twins gathered in the dining-room half an hour later, they were shown a copy of the local paper. Across the front page, in big letters, was the headline:

JANET WESTON CHOSEN QUEEN

Underneath was the picture of the pretty girl they had seen the day before. This was not the real surprise, however. Behind the newly chosen queen were the photographs of four other people. They were the Bobbsey twins!

Scarcely had the children recovered from their surprise over this when Mr. and Mrs. Kape were announced. The friendly couple rushed over to the children, hugged them and congratulated them heartily on having been chosen for the King's court. Mr. and Mrs. Bobbsey were completely surprised.

"Why didn't you tell me about this?" she demanded of the children.

"Why, Mother, we never knew! We thought the King was joking," said Nan. "I'm sure there must be some mistake."

Mr. Kape was about to say that he was sure there was no mistake, when a formal committee of carnival people called to tell the twins.

If Nan and Bert were a little tongue-tied by the honour, not so Freddie and Flossie. The little girl clapped her hands and said excitedly:

"It will be just lovely. What shall I wear? And may my skating dolly be in it too?"

Freddie did handsprings in his joy and toppled over on the last one. He landed with his feet in the empty fireplace!

In fact, everyone was very happy over the honour done the twins except Aunt Sallie Pry. The poor woman was more and more discouraged over the condition of her hotel. Now she was afraid this new popularity of the twins would only add to her troubles.

"Please don't worry, Aunt Sallie," said Nan cheerfully, when the callers had left. "If the Central becomes better known, then more people will come here."

"More guests mean more money for you," added Bert, "and more money gives you a chance to make a better profit."

Since Mrs. Pry was deaf, it was hard for her to find out what was the matter with the hotel. The children decided to do a little investigating on their own account to see why the place was run so poorly.

Here Freddie was very happy, for he rather fancied himself as a detective. The little fellow was all over the place, turning up at the most unexpected times and places. Now and then he would discover a clue that the older children could use.

As they had suspected, Nan and Bert learned that the manager was chiefly to blame for the run-down condition of the hotel. He was a fussy little man who found fault with the servants on small matters and neglected big ones. He had a bad temper and would fly into such rages that no one liked him.

"Aunt Sallie ought to get rid of *him* right away," said Nan to Bert. "And what's more, I'm going to tell her so."

There were others in the hotel who were to blame, too. The chef, for instance, had so many family troubles that he didn't bother much about the cooking. The head waiter was good enough as head waiters go, but the children learned that he had been sick for a long time and really was not fit to work at all.

"Aunt Sally should get healthy, peppy servants," decided Bert.

The children would have had a hard time learning facts about chambermaids and porters, if it had not been for one really pleasant and capable member of the hotel staff. This was Mrs. Tanner, the house-keeper. She was a tall, brisk woman who went about her duties cheerfully. She always seemed to be accompanied by a jingling of keys.

"You are good children to help your aunt," she said pleasantly. "I'll aid you all I can, for I am sorry to see her worried by this place and the shiftless servants in it."

Mrs. Tanner told them that she thought a good

deal of the help should be replaced, and that the sooner they set about it the better. The upshot of all this was that Nan promised to have a good talk with Mrs. Pry just as soon as she could.

The chance came just half an hour later. The Bobbsey girl followed Aunt Sallie into the small room near the lounge which she called her office. Without wasting words, Nan put the whole matter before her.

"I think you should discharge most of the help, Aunt Sallie. Mrs. Tanner—"

"Hammer, hammer, what's that got to do with it?" exclaimed the old lady irritably.

"I said Mrs. Tanner," said Nan patiently, raising her voice. "She says it won't be hard to get a new staff."

"Eh? What did you say? New what?" asked Aunt Sallie, cupping a hand behind her ear.

Once more Nan repeated the sentence. In the end she made the deaf lady understand what she was trying to say.

"Well, all right," agreed the old lady at last, after she learned what the children had found out.

Poor Nan did not know that Danny Rugg had slipped into the lounge while she was talking to Aunt Sallie. He had heard every word she had said! Now he went straight to the office of James Riley, the manager.

Perhaps it was just as well Nan did not know all this. The trouble stirred up by Danny Rugg was going to reach her ears soon enough!

"Everybody ready?" called Mr. Bobbsey early that afternoon. "You haven't forgotten the sleigh ride, have you?"

While the twins waited in the lounge at the Hotel

Windham for Shirley Swift and the other young people, Mr. Bobbsey got into conversation with Mrs. Kape's brother. He owned and managed the hotel. He happened to say something about the servant problem that interested Nan very much. She tucked the information away in her memory, resolved to put it to use for Aunt Sallie at some future time.

"Hi, everybody!" called Shirley as she and her friends flocked into the room.

They gathered up the Bobbsey twins and swept them out to the front of the hotel. There the gaily decorated sleigh was waiting for them.

What fun it was to scramble into the straw at the bottom of it. Then the driver cracked his whip in the air and the horses started off to a merry jingle of bells! The little twins giggled and waved frantically to Mr. Bobbsey as they were whirled around a turn in the road.

The children never forgot that wonderful ride. For more than an hour the horses climbed up and up through the winding mountain passes and gorgeous scenery.

When at last it seemed as if they must have reached the top of the world, the sleigh came to a standstill before a jolly little lodge. It looked as if it might have come straight from a Christmas card.

"This is where we eat," said Shirley, swinging to the ground. "Come on, everybody. I'm starved!"

The lodge was warm inside and smelled deliciously of hot food. The proprietors of the little mountain resort were a pleasant couple who seemed to enjoy the confusion and the noisy high spirits of their young guests.

They bustled about, putting big cups of hot milk on

the long board table and wooden plates heaped with all sorts of food that young people love to eat.

While they were in the midst of this feast, Bert happened to look towards the door. Someone had left it ajar. In the opening stood a large animal, its head lowered, its lips drawn back from wicked teeth.

"A wolf!" shouted the boy. "And he looks hungry."

Bert jumped to his feet, upsetting his stool. It fell over to the floor with a resounding thump.

Others realized their danger in the same instant. The girls shrieked, while the boys picked up their stools or anything they could lay their hands on that might serve as weapons.

"Help! Help!" cried two of the small children, as the animal came on.

In the confusion and excitement the table was upset. All the food, plates and cups went crashing to the floor.

"Freddie! Freddie!"

Bert leaped across the table towards his little brother, who was right in line with the animal.

CHAPTER XIV

DANGER!

FOR a moment Freddie was so frightened that he could not move. Suddenly he felt himself seized by somebody and pulled back violently.

"I'll get him!" yelled the proprietor of the lodge.

He ran for his gun, but the man's wife had a better idea. She seized a large raw steak that had been about to find its way into the frying-pan. She flung it out of the door into the snow.

The animal, confused and dazed, hesitated for a moment. Then he darted through the door after the meat.

Quick as a flash, Bert jumped to the door. He slammed it shut, drawing the wooden staple through the bolt in another second.

It was a moment before the children could realize that the danger was over. Then they crowded to the window. There they saw a large grey animal hungrily devouring the meat.

"Why it's a dog!" Bert exclaimed. "He must have been starving to come charging in like that."

"I was sure it was a wolf," Freddie gasped.

"My good steak," mourned the proprietor. "It was the best steak I had, so juicy, so tender."

"No good will come of moaning, Adolph," said his

104

good wife practically. "Stop now and help us get this place to rights."

The children helped to set up the table again and collect the scattered dishes. By the time they had finished no one would have guessed that there had been such a mess.

On the trip back to the hotel the children went another way, the long way round, driving for some distance through the woods. Here they saw more wild animals, including a glimpse of a lovely, startled deer. But they met none that looked like a wolf.

"Ooo, there's a rabbit!" called Flossie once. "He looked just like an Easter bunny," she added, as the soft furry creature hopped out of sight.

The twins learned from Shirley that various simple events had been arranged for carnival week. In these the young visitors to Fairy Lake might compete. There would be skating, ski-ing and sled races for which all the Bobbseys were eligible.

"Why don't you sign up for some of them?" Shirley urged. "I'm sure you'd have fun."

The twins said they would. Soon afterwards, to their regret, they found themselves nearing the Hotel Windham. This meant the end of the ride.

As they rounded a turn in the narrow road a sleigh going in the opposite direction grazed the runners of their own vehicle. It nearly tilted them into the snow.

"How careless!" cried Shirley Swift.

Bert had caught sight of the passengers in the other sleigh. He called to Nan excitedly.

"Did you see that red-haired fellow? I'm almost sure he was Beany Ferris!"

"And he was with the chef from our hotel," said

Nan. "Now I wonder what that means," she added thoughtfully.

She was not long in finding out that the meeting of the two men meant more trouble for the Central and Aunt Sallie Pry. Mrs. Bobbsey told them all about it when she called for them at the Windham a short time later. After the children had related the pleasant and exciting things that had happened on their sleigh ride, Bert mentioned seeing Beany Ferris and the chef together.

"I'm not surprised," said Mrs. Bobbsey, frowning, as she turned a corner in the slippery road. "Everything is at sixes and sevens at the Central now. All the employees are grumbling. It seems someone has been to them and told them they were going to lose their jobs!"

"Who could have done such a thing?" Nan wondered.

"The manager, James Riley, went to poor Aunt Sallie and asked her point-blank if this was so," continued Mrs. Bobbsey. "Aunt Sallie is so deaf she couldn't understand half he said. Then she got angry and he got angry and they had a dreadful time. I'm sure I don't know what's to be done."

When the children arrived at the Central, they found everything at "sixes and sevens" indeed. Mrs. Pry was in tears. The employees had threatened to leave in a body. The chef had disappeared mysteriously when he should have been preparing the evening meal. In fact, it was hard to see how things ever could get straightened out.

"The place is so cold," said Aunt Sallie. "The furnace man has put on only enough coal to keep the fires from going out."

Without telling anyone Freddie decided he could do something about this. After opening doors and doors he finally found one that led to the cellar. What a mess this was!

"I can't even see the furnace," he said half aloud. "Oh, there it is."

The little fellow also found the coal-bin and started his job. Shovelful after shovelful he put on to the fire, until his poor arms ached. But he did not stop until the fire pit was filled with coal.

He closed the big door and then sat down on the floor. Very tired, he leaned against a pile of rags and fell asleep.

Meanwhile Mrs. Bobbsey had missed her little son. He had been told to take a bath and change his clothes for dinner. Now he was nowhere in sight, so Bert was sent to look for him. After twenty minutes the boy returned.

"I can't find Freddie anywhere," he reported to his mother. "He isn't in the hotel and he isn't out-doors."

"He certainly must be one place or the other," replied Mrs. Bobbsey, worried. "Oh, dear, I guess we'll all have to search for him."

At this point Flossie appeared with a very thin party dress on.

"Why, my child, you'll freeze in that," said her mother. "Put on your white wool dress."

"But it's hot in the hotel," objected Flossie. "It's as hot as—as a fire," she added.

To be sure, it now was very warm in the bedrooms. As Bert realized this, a thought suddenly came into his head. Freddie! Where there might be a fire, there was sure to be the little fireman.

"I bet I can find Freddie!" he called, dashing out of the door.

He had as much trouble finding the cellar as his little brother had. But he did, and there he came upon the sleeping lad.

"Freddie! Freddie!" Bert cried. "Wake up. It's dinner-time. Phew, you're a sight," he added, helping his small brother to his feet.

The little twin was indeed a sight. He was black from head to heels. Now he would need not only a bath but a shampoo as well!

"But I got the hotel warm," he boasted as Bert led him upstairs.

Guests who were appearing for dinner had to laugh at the sight Freddie made. But when they heard what he had done they patted him on the back and said: "You're a big help, little man. Thanks a lot."

The Bobbsey family had to hurry to get to dinner before the dining-room doors closed. But they would not have missed much if they had stayed away, for the evening meal was the worst the guests had had so far at the Central.

Directly afterwards Danny Rugg stopped Nan in the hall. She was just about to enter the lounge on her way to Aunt Sallie's office.

"My mother and father said that was the most awful dinner they had ever had anywhere," said the unpleasant boy, planting himself directly in the girl's way. "A lot of the other guests are complaining, too. I heard them. If there was any other place to go, you wouldn't have anybody in your old hotel."

Nan felt the tears rise to her eyes. At the moment she was suddenly sure that she knew who had spread the ugly report among the employees of the hotel.

"You did it," she accused the bully. "It was you
who went to the chef and the chambermaids and all
the others and told them they were going to lose their
jobs. Wasn't it?"

"Sure. Why not?" said Danny, grinning. "I told
you I'd get even——"

Nan did not wait to hear what more Danny might
have to say. With head high and an angry spot of
colour in her cheeks she went to find her father.

Mr. Bobbsey was having his troubles too. He had
gone to the manager's office to have a talk with the
man about the shiftless management of the hotel.
There he also found the night porter who had greeted
Eric the Red and the other entertainers in such an
unfriendly way on their arrival.

Both hotel men were in an ugly mood. So it happened that Nan, pausing at the door of the office,
heard her father say:

"I came to talk over the situation with you
pleasantly, but if you won't have it so——"

"Pleasant! There's been nothing pleasant about
this hotel since you and that deaf old woman came to
take charge here," the manager flared up. "It's
criticism here, there and everywhere until I can tell
you I'm good and sick of it!"

"And on top of that," said the sullen porter, "we are
told we may be going to lose our jobs."

"You're wrong," said Mr. Bobbsey, and Nan could
tell by her father's voice that he was very angry. "You
are not *going* to lose your jobs. You *have* lost them!
Now get out of here just as soon as you can!"

Mr. Bobbsey was so upset when he came from the
office that he brushed past Nan without seeing her.
His daughter did not stop him.

Inside the office the manager began to talk fast and hard. At the end of it he turned to the porter and commanded:

"Send all the staff to me here at once. If we are to go, they will go with us. I'll see that there's not an employee left in the place! And they can't run the hotel without us!"

CHAPTER XV

THE TWINS TAKE CHARGE

WITH a wildly beating heart, Nan sped along the
corridor. Her first thought was to find her father and
tell him of the manager's threat. She was half-way
down the stairs when an interesting thought popped
into her mind.

What was it she had heard the manager of the
Windham tell her father earlier that day? Something
that she had tucked away in her memory and had
meant to bring out some day when it might be
useful.

"Oh, yes, now I know! Mrs. Kape's brother said
that he is always careful to have extra help on hand
in case of emergency. This is an emergency if ever
there was one! Maybe he'll help us out!"

Downstairs she sped, across the lounge and into
Aunt Sallie's little office. No one was there, but the
place had a telephone and it was the telephone Nan
wanted. She called up the Windham. In her
impatience it seemed a very long time before anyone
answered. But a voice did and she asked to speak to
the manager.

"This is the manager," said a man presently. "Is
there anything—Nan Bobbsey! Yes, of course I
remember you. Mrs. Kape and I have good reason to
remember the Bobbseys, I am sure—and most

delightfully, too. A favour? Why, of cource! Anything I can do——"

Nan poured out her story to the owner of the pleasant voice. She ended with a plea for help in the hard task of getting a new staff for the Central.

"I'm sure Mrs. Tanner, the housekeeper, will stay. She's nice and will help us all she can. But we'll need a chef and some waiters and—oh, dear, I guess we need a little of everything!"

The kindly man promised to do his best for Nan. He could send over a very good cook in the morning and he could let them have three of his own waiters temporarily. As for the other help, there would be no trouble in supplying everything the Bobbseys and Aunt Sallie might need, he was sure. It might take a couple of days, though.

As Nan put down the receiver the little twins peeped around the edge of the door. They looked frightened.

"Oh, Nan, everything is awful out here," said Flossie in tears. "Aunt Sallie is crying again and Daddy is awful mad."

"And all the servants are leaving," said Freddie, big-eyed. "They are coming downstairs now with their suitcases."

Nan hustled the little twins into the lobby and found that Freddie was right. Led by James Riley the entire staff of the Central had gathered at the foot of the stairs, ready to walk out in a body.

Aunt Sallie was in tears and Mrs. Bobbsey had put an arm about her for comfort. Mr. Bobbsey looked on angrily while loyal Mrs. Tanner, the housekeeper, had a final word with the manager. Some of the guests stood about curiously to watch. Suddenly Nan

pushed her way through the group until she stood at
the foot of the stairs.

"It's all right, everybody," she said loudly. "I've
just talked with the manager of the Hotel Windham.
He has promised to send over new servants and a good
chef first thing in the morning."

"I'll say you need them," said a wicked-sounding
voice. It was Danny Rugg! "But probably they won't
come," he added.

Eric the Red, standing near by, turned and looked
hard at Danny. Without another word the unpleasant
boy vanished through a doorway. No doubt he was
afraid of being twisted into a knot!

Every other guest had words of praise for Nan. Mr.
and Mrs. Bobbsey were delighted and even Aunt
Sallie was cheered up at the prospect of having new
help in the hotel.

"We'll do the work until the new people come,"
offered Nan.

As for the little twins, they were excited beyond
words because their wish had come true. They were
to help run a real hotel!

There was plenty for the small Bobbsey children to
do. All that evening they were kept busy going upstairs and downstairs on errands for the guests. Back
and forth they hurried with ice-water, newspapers
and other things as the orders came in. Their little
legs were in danger of being run completely off when
Eric the Red came to the rescue.

"I once worked as a lift boy back in Denver,
Colorado," he joked. "And running a lift is one of
those things a person doesn't forget. So hop in, my
young friends, and I'll give you a real ride."

After that things were easier for the little twins.

Also there was less grumbling among the guests over being forced to use the stairs. Eric the Red was proving himself a good friend in more ways than one.

"And he always seems to enjoy himself doing it," said Mr. Bobbsey in praise of him.

Bert took charge of the desk, answering the telephone and meeting new guests. Nan did double duty, helping in the kitchen and serving on the sweets and magazine counter in the lobby.

"You children ought to go into the hotel business," advised one kindly old gentleman with a smile.

They had reason for being grateful to Mrs. Tanner, too. Without her expert assistance they could not have managed. It was she who rolled up her sleeves and went to work in the kitchen, clearing away the after-dinner dishes and planning the breakfast menu for the following day.

Mrs. Bobbsey helped, of course, but it was Aunt Sallie Pry who was the real surprise to everybody. No longer gloomy or fretful, the old lady was here, there and everywhere, suggesting, supervising, as pert and spry as you please. For the first time since her curious legacy had come to her, she seemed to be really enjoying herself.

"Having fun, Aunt Sallie?" asked Nan on one of her trips to the kitchen.

"On the run?" repeated Mrs. Pry briskly. "I should say so, but I like it. Maybe we'll make a go of this place, now that we've got rid of that James Riley and his awful tribe. Riff-raff, every one of them!"

What's more, Aunt Sallie's cheerfulness lasted. She was up before any of them in the morning and was busy making the coffee before even Mrs. Tanner appeared. Breakfast was a bit slow, but everyone—

with the exception of the Rugg family—agreed that it was the best one they had had yet at the Central.

"It's funny the chef didn't come back," said Mrs. Tanner. "He had a day off yesterday, but he wasn't discharged."

No one had seen the fellow, it seemed, since the glimpse Bert and Nan had had of him in the sleigh with Beany Ferris. This set Bert to wondering again about Beany. Had the thief been caught or had he once more got away from the police?

Directly after breakfast Mr. Kape came over in response to a telephone call from Bert. The two set out to trace the thief and if possible find an answer to the boy's questions.

The hotel, under its new "management", was in full swing when members of the new staff began to arrive. And how different they were from James Riley and his friends! Willing to work and cheerful, they fitted right into the new scheme of things. Before the morning was half over the hotel was humming with activity.

Lucky for the twins it was, too, for about mid-morning they received the exciting news that the King and Queen of the Carnival were coming to lunch. Directly afterwards they would "grant an audience to the members of their new Court".

Then, indeed, there *was* some planning to do!

"This is our chance to make the Central shine," Nan said happily. "There isn't time to get new chairs for the lobby, but we can fix up the place so it will look better. Mrs. Tanner says there are some flowered slip covers we can put on the furniture to make it seem as good as new."

"And Daddy has ordered flowers to be put in the

lounge in honour of the King and Queen," said Flossie, breathless with excitement. "Oh, Nan, it will look bee-utiful."

And indeed by the time the "royalty" were due to arrive this was true. Here was a new, bright, friendly hotel that looked as little like the bleak old Central as it was possible to imagine. At Flossie's suggestion they had even changed its name to Central Palace!

"I can hardly wait," said the little girl over and over again.

For once everything went well. Nan had planned the menu—a clear soup, tiny fish-balls in parsley sauce, a frozen fruit salad trimmed with watercress and lettuce. The main course was to consist of individual steaks, small potatoes, and beans. For dessert there would be ice-cream and tiny macaroons. The macaroons were Aunt Sallie's speciality, and the old lady's pride in the ones she made was very pleasant to see.

While Freddie was carrying piles of clean linen to the dining-room and Flossie was arranging the lettuce on small plates, Bert came in from his trip with Mr. Kape. Nothing had been learned about Beany Ferris, he reported.

"We hope that the police will turn up a clue soon," he said wearily.

Nan, rushing about to make sure that everything would be ready in time for luncheon, begged her twin to go to the help of the new receptionist.

"He seems to be having trouble with the keys. Do find out what's wrong, Bert," she pleaded anxiously.

The Bobbsey boy soon discovered what was wrong. In the absence of the receptionist, Danny Rugg was behind the counter deliberately mixing up the keys!

"Stop that!" cried Bert.

He made a dash for Danny, but the bully was too quick for him. He dodged around the counter and out among a group of people where Bert could not follow him without making a great disturbance.

"I'll get even with him later," the Bobbsey boy vowed as he arranged the keys in their boxes.

But Danny was not done with his mischief. He was determined to cause the twins as much trouble as possible. To make their party to the King and Queen a failure if it could be done, he coaxed a dirty and frightened stray dog into the lobby.

People moved aside. One or two of the men tried to shoo the creature outside, but the animal would not move back. Instead, he growled and showed his teeth. Danny stood in the doorway, waving his arms and urging the tormented beast farther into the hotel.

"Do get that dog out of here!" cried Nan desperately. "If the King and Queen should come now, everything will be spoiled."

That, of course, was just what Danny wanted. The dog, however, had other ideas. A man suddenly tapped him with a cane and the terrified animal decided to run outside.

Danny was directly in his path. In confusion the animal leaped at the boy, nipping him in the arm. Then as the bully whirled about, bawling, the dog took a firm grip on the lad's pants. There was a sharp sound of tearing as a good part of the cloth came away! Yelling and blubbering, Danny jumped down the porch steps two at a time. Meanwhile the dog disappeared around the side of the hotel.

None too soon, either. At that moment a car drew up before the door and from it stepped the King and Queen of the Carnival!

CHAPTER XVI

FIRST PRIZE

THE Bobbsey twins held their breaths. This was one of the biggest affairs they had ever planned.

"Hallo! Hallo!" the handsome King said to the children.

"Hallo, my dears," added the Queen, hugging Freddie.

Now the little boy might have blushed at this attention in front of so many people, but just now he was too excited to care. He had planned a surprise all on his own account.

Without saying anything to anyone, the boy had spoken to some of the musicians staying at the hotel. He had begged them to play a jolly piece when the "royalty" should arrive. Asked what he would like Freddie had replied:

"My favourite tune is Jingle Bells."

So now as the King and Queen came to the door of the dining-room, the orchestra started this lively air with a will. All the guests, entering into the spirit of the festive occasion, began to sing, until the whole dining-room was ringing with their voices.

After that gay beginning the luncheon was bound to be a great success. The King and Queen were the pleasantest young people imaginable, besides being the handsomest, Flossie was sure.

They exclaimed over the luncheon and seemed to enjoy everything immensely. The macaroons came in for special mention. Nan was sure the Queen made a friend of Aunt Sallie for life by praising them and asking for the recipe.

After the meal was over the twins learned just what would be expected of them at the carnival. It all sounded very thrilling.

"You will ride in the float with us," said the King, "as part of our court. We shall have rehearsals for that later, of course."

"And you will have the most gorgeous costumes," the Queen added. "All white, sparkling with sequins. Your hats will be white, too, with long, curling blue plumes."

"And what will you wear?" asked Flossie, big-eyed.

"Oh, ermine, of course, as becomes royalty," laughed the Queen.

"Somebody said the film companies would take pictures for the newsreels. Is that true?" asked Bert.

"Oh, there will be lots of cameramen about," King Victor Comstock agreed, laughing. "You will find yourselves very famous before the carnival is over."

"It will be swell advertising for the Central Palace, anyway," said Bert and everybody laughed at the practical thought.

It was Freddie who, without meaning to, provided the best advertising for Aunt Sallie's inheritance, however. This is the way it happened.

Tiring of the talk about the carnival, the little boy wandered out into the lobby. There he met a nice young man who instantly began to talk to him. Now Freddie did not know that the nice young man was a newspaper reporter. The boy spoke to him quite openly about Mrs. Pry's unusual legacy. He told him all about their troubles with the servants and the fun they were having trying to run the hotel themselves.

"That is a great story," said the young man.

It must have appealed to him very much, for the next day it appeared as a feature article in his newspaper under the large-type heading:

AUNT SALLIE'S INHERITANCE

Mr. Bobbsey laughed when he saw the story. "The Central Palace certainly is getting a good deal of publicity, thanks to my children!" he remarked.

The next day was the start of the first events of the Ice Carnival. Eric the Red was entered in the ski jump and the twins had promised to be on hand early to cheer for him.

The weather was perfect for winter sports: clear and cold, with a crispy crust to the snow that made walking on it fun. The children reached the highest and longest of the ski jumps just as the first event was to begin.

Mr. Bobbsey was already there and had kept a place for them so they were able to get a good view of the entertainment. Several contenders for the title came before Eric the Red.

The children watched breathlessly as these expert skiers whizzed down the steep incline and took off into space, arms spread for balance and knees bent for contact with the hard-packed ground. There were one or two spills but most of the jumps were successful and won hearty applause from the watchers.

"There comes Eric! Hurrah!" shouted Freddie.

At the top of the slope, his blond-red hair vivid against the white background, the young man paused a moment. Then down he came, zooming through the air while the twins cheered themselves hoarse. He made a perfect landing, sweeping around in a long arc before the judges' stand.

"That was a swell jump. I bet he wins," Bert cried in glee.

"I'm glad I wasn't on his shoulders that time," laughed Flossie.

Eric the Red did win the event. What was more, although the children did not know it at the time, he had broken a world's record as well!

The twins could not wait to congratulate Eric, for Mr. Bobbsey had entered the little ones in the small sled races. As the first of these was scheduled to start in a few minutes, the youngsters had to rush to get ready.

The race was over a short course but it was fairly steep and had several rather sharp turns. Now that the moment was at hand they were a little nervous and waited anxiously for the starting-gun.

"I hope you both win!" cried Bert.

Pop! There was the crack of the pistol. And there were Freddie and Flossie going down the steep incline and keeping well ahead of the other contestants.

Around the curves they went, guiding their little sleds expertly, while people yelled and cheered on the sidelines. Once Freddie got into trouble with his steering-gear. For one awful moment it looked as if he might dive head-first into a snowbank! But he straightened out in the nick of time and came home to a roaring finish.

The result of the race was that Freddie won first prize for the boys and Flossie for the girls! Bert had had his wish come true.

"Let me see your prizes," said Nan as the little twins came up to them.

Freddie's face was beaming. "Flossie's only got a silly old doll. But I got a fire-engine," the little boy cried. "And it will run, too, all by itself."

When these prizes had been admired by all, the crowd moved on to the part of Fairy Lake where the exhibition skating was to take place. As they reached the spot, a pretty young figure, dressed in a dazzling short white costume, flashed out on the ice. It swooped towards the Bobbseys in a long, graceful glide.

"That's Shirley in her exhibition of figure skating. Now we'll really see something," said Nan, pressing forward to the very edge of the ice.

There was repeated applause from the watchers as the girl skater twisted and whirled in several clever designs. Then the music started and she began to waltz.

After a moment or two it was noticed that the clever young skater seemed to be in trouble. Her movements became less sure and her hands seemed to be fumbling with something at her waist.

"Oh!" cried Nan. "Her sash! It's coming loose!"

The long ribbon threatened to fall at any moment about Shirley's ankles and trip her! As the young skater neared the Bobbsey group, the Bobbsey girl ran out on the ice. Quickly she seized the flying end of the loosened sash and gave it a sharp tug. The cloth came away in her hands. Shirley, free, whirled away with a nod and a smile of thanks.

"That was good work, Nan," applauded Mr. Bobbsey.

"Yes, quick thinking. It probably saved Shirley a nasty spill," Bert added in praise.

The young skater finished her number amid hearty handclapping from the audience. Other performers followed her, but none, it seemed to them, was as good.

Shirley was entered in another event, an "acrobatic dance on skates". Others came first, but when Shirley appeared at last she was greeted with greater acclaim than anyone. She did beautifully, too, for there was no troublesome sash to get in her way this time.

Sure that she would be mentioned for an award, the Bobbseys moved towards the judges' stand, the better to hear the verdict. They had guessed correctly. Shirley was awarded first prize!

Just as the chairman was announcing the other winners, someone threw a snowball over the heads of the crowd. The ball, packed hard and solid, struck the judge squarely on the bridge of the nose!

"I bet Danny Rugg did that," said Freddie excitedly. "I just saw him sneaking away from here."

Whether or not Danny Rugg was the culprit, as Freddie seemed to believe, it was certain that the judge was in no condition to continue his duties. While he retired to nurse his bruised nose, a hasty search was made for a substitute judge. Mr. Bobbsey, now famous as the father of the two sets of twins, was pounced upon and coaxed into the position.

"Well," he laughed, "if you'll let my children help to advise me, I'll do it."

It was great fun to assist their father in making important decisions. Once more Danny Rugg had done the twins a favour when he had tried to do them harm! The unpleasant boy grew more jealous than ever over the twins' increasing popularity. He set himself to thinking up new ways to get even with them.

"The next time it will work," he vowed.

That night a lovely party was held at the Central Palace. The place was crowded now, due to interest in the Ice Carnival, in the twins being part of the court, and the new, intelligent management.

A huge open fire burned in the lounge and the children had brought armfuls of sweet-smelling boughs to fling on the blaze. In this cosy setting they passed around nuts and apples to the guests.

After a day in the open nothing could be more delightful than an evening spent in this way. Everyone, relaxed and happy, reviewed the events of the day, swapping stories that filled the place with gay laughter. Through it all Flossie floated in her best "princess" manner. No wonder the Central Palace was fast becoming the most popular meeting-place at Fairy Lake!

"It's too good to be true. I'm afraid I'll wake up," said Aunt Sallie Pry, "and find it was a dream."

"It's really true," replied Nan, happy that at last the old lady was enjoying her inheritance.

The next day was to be a thrilling one for Nan and Bert. They were to compete in the skating races at the lake for children of their age. The competition would be stiff, they knew, for some of the best among the visiting skaters had been entered for the event.

"If you beat me," Nan told her twin just before the start, "I'll—I'll—"

What she was going to say Bert never found out, for a man began to give directions and everyone else stopped talking. Bert looked across at his sister and grinned.

"I'm going to do my best," his eyes told her.

The starter gave the preliminary warning and the

skaters leaned forward, ears ready for the crack of the pistol.

There was a report and the young people leaped forward, skates striking sparks from the ice. Off they went like the wind!

CHAPTER XVII

THE STOLEN HANDBAG

THE little twins watched eagerly while brother and sister flew down the course. There were four others besides Nan and Bert, two boys and two girls in the race. For some time they all kept fairly even. Then the Bobbsey boy began to forge ahead.

"Where's Nan? I don't see Nan at all!" cried Freddie, trying to peer over the head of a much larger boy in front of him.

"She's in fourth place now, but she's moving up," said Mr. Bobbsey. He lifted his little son on to his shoulder so that he could see over the heads of the crowd. "That better?"

Here Flossie demanded to be taken up, too, so her father put her on his other shoulder.

"My, my," he laughed. "You fatties must have been eating a lot of heavy food."

Bert led the others nearly all the way. Towards the end one of the other boys caught up with him and skated abreast of him for a while. Gradually the Bobbsey boy pulled out. He was a good half-length ahead at the finishing-line.

"Bert won! My brother won!" shouted Flossie excitedly.

Flossie was divided between joy at Bert's success and pity for Nan, who had finished a rather poor third.

"But she beat the rest of the girls and one of the boys!" her little sister said loyally.

Any chagrin Nan might have felt over her failure in the race was more than made up later in the day. Word was sent to the Central Palace asking her to take the place of a girl who was to have presented the King of the Carnival with a Diamond Key. The girl was sick, the message said, and Nan had been chosen in her place.

She accepted joyfully and was taken that afternoon to the Hotel Windham to rehearse her part. The other Bobbseys went back to Fairy Lake, unable to tear themselves away from the delights of the carnival.

The merriment was in full swing now. There were crowds everywhere. Men selling food and novelties walked about among the pleasure-seekers.

"I like that jolly man with the big apron and the big hat," said Flossie.

And what little girl wouldn't have liked such a person? He had a wonderful smile and he kept singing all the time.

"He's like the picture man in my book at home," went on Flossie to her twin. "Only he puts different words to the song."

"Oh—o—o—o—o," the fellow cried,
"Some like 'em hot,
Some like 'em cold,
But nobody likes 'em
When they're too old.

Come and get my fresh frankfurters!" he called loudly.

Flossie giggled and hoped the man would sing some more. But he did not, so she turned away just in time to see Danny Rugg coming towards her. Something about the way the boy looked made her think he was up to some mischief. But she didn't suppose he meant to play a trick on her. Yet that was exactly the young bully's idea.

"Oh," screamed the little girl suddenly, "he's taken my dolly! My lovely skating dolly!"

The boy had indeed grabbed Flossie's precious Christmas present from her arm. Away he raced with it towards Fairy Lake. Once there, he set the doll down on the ice and spun her round and round. One skate came off and then the tiny cap.

"I get him! I get him!" cried the jolly frankfurter man, running on to the ice.

Then was Danny sorry he had been such a mean boy! For the big man not only took the doll away from him, but turned the lad over his knee and spanked him!

"Oh, thank you so much," said Flossie, as the bully slunk away and she hugged her dolly once more.

A few minutes after this the little twins were admiring a merry-go-round built of snow animals. Suddenly Bert saw a familiar face in the crowd. The sandy eyebrows and deep-set eyes could belong to no one but Beany Ferris!

"Stay here!" Bert told the little twins hastily. "I'll be right back!"

By this time the thief had disappeared. Bert thought he had lost him. After a moment he caught sight of the fellow again, however, and followed along, hoping to find a policeman.

Suddenly Beany bumped into a well-dressed woman, brushing against her so roughly that she almost fell. The lady cried out and clutched at the man to steady herself. The fellow pretended to help her but was very clumsy about it. As Bert ran up, Beany Ferris disappeared in the crowd.

"My handbag is gone!" cried the woman suddenly. "It was snatched from my arm. That man did it! Stop thief! Stop thief!"

By this time a crowd had gathered. Bert tried to explain that he knew the man who had stolen her handbag but the woman was too excited to listen.

"I believe you helped him," she said, pointing at Bert. "Hold that boy, officer!" she demanded as a man in uniform pushed his way through the crowd.

"And what's he been doin'?" asked the policeman, taking a firm grip of Bert's collar. "Pocket-picking, did you say?"

"He stole my handbag. It had my railway ticket in it, besides seventy-five dollars and a valuable necklace. You must make him give it back at once, officer," said the woman.

Now Freddie and Flossie had been attracted by the noise and confusion and had come to see what it was all about. The little boy was so alarmed at seeing Bert in the grip of a policeman that he ran off as fast as he could to get help. Fortunately he had not gone far when he saw Mr. and Mrs. Kape.

"Oh, come quick!" the little boy gasped out. "Bert's in trouble. I'm afraid he's got to go to prison."

Not knowing what to expect, the couple hurried over to the excited group.

"Mr. Kape," cried Bert, breaking away from the policeman and running up to his friend, "please tell these people that I haven't stolen anything! They think I took this lady's handbag but it was Beany Ferris who did it!"

"You've seen Beany Ferris?" Mr. Kape returned with quick interest.

"Yes, sir. I was following him when he bumped into this lady and stole her handbag," said Bert. "That is," he added honestly, "I'm almost sure he stole it, though I didn't see him do it."

After that it took only a few minutes to convince both the policeman and the woman that the Bobbsey boy had nothing to do with the theft. Mr. Kape explained about Beany Ferris. The policeman said he had heard of the fellow and promised to do all he could to capture the thief.

The woman apologized to Bert for her suspicions and asked the boy to shake hands as a sign that there was no ill-feeling on either side. As Bert held out his hand, the woman gave a glance at her own. Suddenly she gasped out in dismay:

"My diamond ring is gone! My beautiful ring!"

Victor Comstock, King of the Ice Carnival, happened to be passing at that moment and paused for a word with his friends. After speaking to Mr. and Mrs. Kape and the twins, he turned to the woman who had been robbed.

"Hallo, Aunt Eleanor. Anything the matter? You look put out about something!"

"Put out! I guess you would look put out, too, Victor Comstock, if you had just lost a purse and a valuable diamond ring!" said the lady sharply. "It isn't any joke, I can tell you!"

The King said soothingly that he was sure it was not. He promised to do all in his power to find his relative's property.

It would be hard to say who was the more surprised: the twins to find the woman was related to the King; or the woman to find that the King was a friend of the twins! At any rate, Victor Comstock's formal introduction of the Bobbseys as members of his court seemed to impress the rich lady. From that time on she was much more cordial to the children, even inviting them to visit her some time while they were at Fairy Lake.

By this time the youngsters were rather tired from all the excitement. When Mr. Kape offered to drop them off at the Central Palace on his way home, they accepted readily.

"Oh, Bert," cried Nan, rushing up to her twin as he stepped into the hotel, "when I got back from the Windham, I heard some dreadful news."

"What is it?" asked Bert.

"Who do you think was here only an hour ago? That awful man who used to be manager, James Riley. He means to make trouble!"

CHAPTER XVIII

FREDDIE'S TRICK

THE children had forgotten about James Riley. Nothing had been heard from any member of the staff since the night they had walked out of the Central in a body. Certainly no one expected them to make trouble.

"What happened? What did Aunt Sallie tell him?" Bert asked.

"She didn't see him because her lawyer was here, but he told me he was coming back again and 'have it out' with Aunt Sallie," said Nan with a worried look. "Daddy and Mother aren't here and I—I was getting a little frightened," the girl confessed.

"Well, you needn't be frightened any more," said Freddie, going over to his sister protectingly. "Bert and I will take care of you, won't we, Bert?"

His brother said "Sure thing!" and Nan hugged Freddie. Neither of them, however, took Freddie's words seriously, until much later, when they found out just how much he *had* helped!

Mr. and Mrs. Bobbsey had not returned, and Mrs. Sallie Pry was still talking with her lawyer when James Riley made his second visit to the Central Palace.

Guests were beginning to return from the day's sports so the lobby was fairly crowded when the former manager pushed his way in. He approached the desk noisily.

Bert was taking charge while the regular receptionist was away on other duties. He looked up just as James Riley reached the counter.

"Who's in charge here?" demanded the fussy little man sharply. "I want to speak to someone in authority."

Bert came around the desk hastily and tried to lead his unwelcome visitor into an adjoining room. But James Riley would not budge.

"Who's in charge?" he all but shouted while people began to turn and stare at him curiously.

"I am," said Bert. "At least, I'm taking care of things just now. I'll call Mrs. Pry," he added, "just as soon as she's through talking with her lawyer."

"You can tell her she owes me some money," said the unpleasant man in a voice that could be heard from one end of the lobby to the other. "And I want it, too! I'm not going to be put off this time."

It was here that Freddie came to the rescue of his elder brother. He made his way through the crowd and tugged at Mr. Riley's coat.

"Eh?" said the man, looking down at the small lad. "What do you want?"

"Come with me," said the little boy, beckoning mysteriously and moving towards the stairs. "I'll fix things for you."

Riley looked uncertain but followed Freddie after a moment's hesitation. He supposed he was going to be led to Mrs. Pry. Nan and Bert watched this performance curiously.

"*What* do you suppose he's up to?" the girl whispered to her twin.

Bert shook his head wonderingly. "Haven't a notion," he admitted. "Anyway, it gives us time to talk to Aunt Sallie."

"That's right. We can put her on her guard," nodded Nan. "Good old Freddie!"

Meanwhile the little boy had led the man to the bedroom he shared with Bert. With the same mysterious look he pushed open the door and pointed.

"In there," he said.

James Riley looked a little puzzled. For a moment Freddie thought he was going to refuse to enter. Then, with an angry exclamation the man shoved the door open and stepped inside the room.

Now this was just what Freddie had hoped for. He quickly reached for the knob. Before the astonished manager knew what was happening, the little boy had pulled the door shut, locking it on the outside!

"You rascal!" shouted the man.

Chuckling to himself, the little fellow drew the key from the lock. Then he scampered off to tell his brother and sister what he had done!

Meanwhile, Bert and Nan had made good use of the few moments Freddie had given them. Mrs. Pry had almost finished her talk with the lawyer when they burst in upon her with their story.

It was not easy to make the old lady understand what they were trying to tell her. When they finally did she said she was sure James Riley was in the wrong.

"Your father went over the books with me," she said, "and everything that was owing the employees up to the time they walked out of here was sent to them."

"Just to make sure, we'd better go over the files

again," the lawyer suggested. "I can tell by a glance at them whether this fellow's claims are any good."

A look at the books was enough to satisfy the lawyer that Aunt Sallie and Mr. Bobbsey had been right. The Central Palace owed James Riley nothing at all!

It was at this moment that Freddie came running in. He told of the trick he had played on the unfortunate man.

"Good for you!" Aunt Sallie nodded briskly. "It's no more than he deserves, coming here to demand money nobody owes him. I'm glad you locked him up."

"He was awful mad," said Freddie, remembering the shouts and kicks on the door that he had heard all the way downstairs.

"Eh? Awful bad? I suppose he must be," said Aunt Sallie and shook her head sadly over James Riley's wickedness.

She, the lawyer, and the Bobbsey children went upstairs together to release the prisoner. Thanks to the time Freddie had gained for them, they were able to tell the furious man that he was wrong, as the books showed.

The lawyer added a word of warning about people who broke into other folks' property and the awful things that were apt to happen to them, if they made charges that they couldn't back up.

James Riley departed, muttering something about "getting a lawyer". He looked wicked and ugly still, but somehow the children felt that they need have no further fear of him. Thanks to Freddie, they were rid of this mean person for good.

Aunt Sallie was so grateful to the twins for all they

had done for her since coming to Moosehead that she decided to do something for them in return. So the next morning she led them up to the top of the hotel and opened the door of a small storeroom under the eaves.

"I haven't looked in here very thoroughly," she said, "but it seems to me that there are a great many things in this place to interest young people. Look them over, anyway, and if there is anything you'd like, help yourselves."

"You mean—we may keep anything we find?" demanded Flossie, big-eyed.

"Mind? Of course I don't mind. Just help your-selves," said Aunt Sallie. With a nod and a smile she left them.

Their kind friend could have thought of no finer reward for the children. This little storeroom was like a treasure cave to them. Joyfully they set to work to explore its mysteries.

Bert found something exciting right away; a large toy ice-boat, which must have been, at some time or other, the joy and delight of its original owner. The boat was in fairly good shape. Its rigging needed a little repair work and the paint had been scraped off here and there, but the damage was slight.

Bert settled himself on a three-legged stool near the window, took out his penknife, a ball of cord, and set to work. He whistled happily.

"Look over here," cried Freddie, rummaging in a corner. "I've found a box of paints and a lot of brushes. And, oh my, here are pictures, too, lots of them!"

Sure enough, the little boy had found the treasure of some amateur painter. The artist had liked the scenery around Fairy Lake apparently, for there were several wintry scenes which the children recognized easily. There was one blank canvas, too. This made Freddie want to try his hand with the palette and paint brushes.

"I bet I can make a better picture than these, too," said the little boy hopefully. "You just wait and see."

Meanwhile, Nan and Flossie had discovered an interesting old trunk tucked way back around a pile of old furniture. They dragged it out to the light and explored its contents eagerly.

"Oh, look at these bee-autiful things!" exclaimed Flossie.

There were bits of silk and velvet which the little girl wanted for new clothes for her dolly. Two large squares of lace Nan said would make pretty covers for pillows for her room at home.

Suddenly Flossie made a real find. She picked up a heavy photograph album from the trunk. As the little girl tried to lift it, she found it was too heavy for her. The old velvet-covered book slipped from her chubby hands and a letter fell from among the leaves.

It was a fat, important-looking letter. As Flossie tried to spell out the writing on the envelope, Nan came to look over her shoulder.

"Why, it's some sort of deed, I think," said the older girl with sudden excitement. "I saw one that Daddy had once. He said it's what you get from a lawyer when you own property. And look, it's addressed to John Pry. That must be Aunt Sallie's nephew who died and left her this hotel. Oh, isn't it exciting? Maybe this deed means some more inheritance for Aunt Sallie!"

"Let's go down and ask Dad about it," Bert proposed. "I saw him come in from the lake a little while ago."

So down the twins trooped to find their father and show him what they had discovered. Mr. Bobbsey said the paper looked legal enough. Possibly Mrs. Pry would get another legacy!

"I'd rather consult the lawyer before I say anything to Aunt Sallie about it, though," he added. "It would be too bad to raise her hopes, perhaps for nothing."

The children would have asked to go with Mr. Bobbsey to see the lawyer, but they remembered a promise they had made. They were to meet Eric the Red at Fairy Lake before the regular races were to begin. The skier had given them a thrilling invitation. He had asked them to take a sail with him in his iceboat!

"I can watch how he does it," said Bert. "Then I'll know how to run my toy one."

When they arrived at the lake, the twins found to their disgust that Danny Rugg and his father had hired a boat. The two were cruising around in it.

"I hope that mean boy won't make trouble," said Freddie.

CHAPTER XIX

NAN'S IDEA

THE twins forgot about Danny when Eric the Red hailed them. They scrambled aboard his trim craft and shouted with delight as the wind caught the sail and they scudded off down the lake.

"Whee-ee, watch your heads!" yelled Bert. "Here we go!"

It was a lovely feeling to skim along the ice, scarcely seeming to touch it at all! Eric the Red managed the sail so skilfully that every bit of breeze was caught, held, and made the most of.

The Bobbseys were having a glorious time when a second boat zoomed up beside them. In it were Danny and Mr. Rugg. The boy waved and shouted a challenge.

"Bet we beat you!" he yelled.

As luck would have it, a sharp gust of wind filled the sail of the Bobbseys' boat just then, heeling it over dangerously. In the excitement the little twins leaned too far to one side. With a slither and scrape, the boat capsized, spilling them all out on the ice!

Away they went in every direction. Freddie turned over and over before he finally came to rest against a bank of snow. Nan clutched Flossie and broke her fall, so that the little girl was more shaken up than hurt. Neither of the older twins had more than a bruise to show for the accident.

"Ho, ho, ho!" cried Danny. "You look so funny. Some sailors, you are!"

The twins took the spill as part of the fun of the ride. When Eric the Red righted his craft they climbed aboard laughingly and continued the sail. But they paid no attention to Danny.

They had a wonderful time, but on the way home the bully caught up with them again. He waved teasingly.

"Whoever said you could sail an ice-boat?" he jeered.

"We'll never hear the end of that," Bert sighed as they glided in to their moorings.

"Oh, well, who cares what Danny Rugg thinks? We had a good time, anyway," said Freddie sturdily.

Bert was right. The bully seemed determined not to let the twins forget the accident on the ice. Wherever they went the unpleasant boy managed to turn up, a mean smile on his face and a remark about their poor sailing always on his lips.

One day, to escape him, Nan and Bert decided to go ski-ing along one of the mountain trails. They had come down one of the steep hills and up the incline on the farther side and now leaned against a rough log building to rest. Suddenly they heard voices they recognized.

Victor Comstock, the King of the Carnival, was talking to someone whose voice they easily recognized. It was that of his Queen, lovely Janet Weston.

"This is a wonderful place," the King was saying. "You know, Janet, if I could find the right kind of business, I'd like nothing better than to settle down here for good."

"That would be nice," said the girl softly.

"Would *you* like it? Do you think you could be happy here?" the young man asked eagerly.

Nan and Bert exchanged laughing glances and moved off along the trail again.

"So they're beginning to like each other," mused Nan. "Bert, I wonder——"

"What?" asked her brother as she paused.

"The King said something about finding a business and settling down here at Fairy Lake. Do you suppose he might like to buy Aunt Sallie's hotel? That would be a good business for him, now that it's running so well."

"We can talk to Aunt Sallie about it, anyway," agreed Bert. "Whee-ee, look at that hill," he added, as they came to a smooth, white sweep of snow. "Race you, Nan!"

Down the twins rushed, their bodies bent against the rush of wind, the tassels of their scarves streaming out behind them. Wonder of wonders, the two of them got to the bottom at the very same moment.

That afternoon all four children went with their mother on an errand of mercy to a big white building high in the hills. In it were a number of crippled children.

"They can't skip and run and jump the way you can," Mrs. Bobbsey had said, "so I think it would be a good idea for you to give one afternoon to trying to make them a little happier, don't you?"

The children had agreed, of course. So now, with baskets of good things from Aunt Sallie's hotel kitchen and a few of their own toys, they set out for the big white building on the hill.

The hospital was a cheerful place inside, airy and

clean. There were many tall windows through which the sun streamed cheerfully.

Rows of little cots stood side by side and white, eager children's faces were turned to the twins as they went up and down the long room. They gave out all Aunt Sallie's goodies and now and then left one of the toys on a bedside tray. There were not nearly enough toys or goodies to go around, so the Bobbseys promised to return another day with more gifts.

One of the little girls asked shyly for a song. The nurse explained that the children loved music and that visitors rarely were able to get away without singing for them.

"We don't sing very well," said Flossie, but this made no difference.

So Mrs. Bobbsey went to a small white piano in one corner of the long room and struck a chord. The twins sang together several pieces they had learned in school. They had good voices and sang well, though now and then one of the little twins would go out of tune.

No one seemed to mind, however, and when the little concert was over all the sick children applauded heartily. They looked so much brighter and happier than when the twins had come, that the Bobbseys were very glad they had made the visit.

They were a little silent on the way home. When Freddie said he supposed it was a good thing they had gone to cheer up the sick children, Mrs. Bobbsey hugged him and replied:

"I'm glad you feel that way, Freddie. I want *my* children always to remember those who are less fortunate than themselves."

That evening Nan and Bert told the rest of their

family and Mrs. Pry about the conversation they had heard that morning between the King and the Queen of the Carnival. Flossie and Freddie were particularly interested.

"I'm sure a King would have lots of money and could buy Aunt Sallie's hotel without any trouble," said the little boy.

"Probably the Queen would like to come here and run the Central Palace after her own Ice Palace is melted," Flossie added.

Aunt Sallie thought Nan's idea certainly was worth looking into. "I'll have a word with Victor Comstock as soon as I find the time," she said.

The next day the children met Shirley Swift at Fairy Lake. Nan invited her friend to a supper-party that night at Mrs. Pry's hotel. The young skater accepted with pleasure. Then she asked the twins if they would like to learn a few fancy steps.

"Oh, we'd love it!" cried Nan. "Do you think you could really teach us some of the things you can do?"

"Of course I can. Why not? First of all, I'll show you the figure eight. That's easiest," returned Shirley. "See, this is how it's done."

With a flash of her skates and a dizzying double loop, she cut a perfect figure eight in the ice.

"Now you try it," she coaxed.

It was one thing to watch Shirley do it, and quite another to do it themselves the twins soon found out. They had lots of fun trying, however, and Nan and Bert were quick to learn. Even the little twins, though they sat down on the ice too often for comfort, in a short while could cut a wavering and wobbling figure eight.

That afternoon, hearing that some films of the

carnival were to be shown at the local cinema, the children begged to be allowed to go. Mr. Bobbsey said he would drive them over. Also he would call for them after the show, so that they could get back to the hotel in plenty of time for the supper-party.

The feature picture was showing when the twins reached the cinema. They settled themselves to enjoy it while waiting for the scenes of the Ice Carnival. At last the first glimpse of Fairy Lake was thrown on the screen. Bert and Nan sat up alertly. The little twins pushed forward to the very edges of their seats.

"There's Eric the Red in the ski jump!" cried Freddie.

"We must be off in the crowd there somewhere," Nan said. "Wouldn't it be funny if we should see ourselves?"

Then they did see themselves! The scene changed to show the Queen of the Carnival. There in the background, peeping around a group of other people were the four Bobbsey twins, just as plain as could be!

Flossie was so excited she fell forward on to the floor. In turning to help her, Bert made an important discovery. Seated in the second row behind them, sound asleep, was the red-haired man they had come to know as Beany Ferris!

Quietly, making a sign to Nan to keep the little twins where they were, Bert slipped into the aisle and went in search of an attendant. He was determined to have the thief arrested before he could slip away from him again!

"Now's my chance," he thought.

CHAPTER XX

THE PARTY

TO Bert's surprise and chagrin, the attendant refused to do anything about Beany Ferris.

"I can't have him arrested," he insisted stubbornly. "It would mean a row and the audience would be disturbed. Probably I would be discharged."

Desperate now for fear Beany would escape while he was arguing with this fellow, Bert asked to see the manager.

"He isn't in the cinema," the attendant told the boy impatiently, adding, "You'd better go back to your seat now and stop making so much noise. People are beginning to wonder what's wrong."

Not knowing what else to do, Bert went back into the cinema, only to find that Beany Ferris's seat was empty. Once more the thief had got out of sight!

All through the rest of the show Bert was gloomy, thinking of the chance he had missed. The only bright idea about it was that the man still was in the vicinity.

He cheered up when the twins reached the Central Palace, however, for party preparations were in full swing. Everybody seemed very gay.

Mrs. Bobbsey had been to town and returned with gifts that looked like snowballs but weren't. She said they were to give them all a surprise later on.

"Here comes Shirley," announced Nan presently, and ran to meet the young skater.

There were whispers of "Oh, isn't she pretty?" from the other diners as the girl made her way to the Bobbsey's table. Eric the Red had been invited to the table too. He got up to make Shirley a graceful little speech, bidding her welcome to the Central Palace.

The girl responded prettily, and there was a burst of clapping from all over the room. Everyone seemed to be having a good time except Danny Rugg. The boy sat at a corner table with his parents and kept his eyes sulkily on his plate.

"How he hates to see anyone having fun!" thought Nan. "I wish sometimes he would join in."

The party supper proved to be a great success, from the snowball gifts, which were hollow and filled with sweets, to the big cake with "Welcome Shirley Swift" written on its top in pink icing.

As they were finishing their meal, Bert gave Eric the Red a sign. The man nodded and got to his feet.

"Ladies and gentlemen," he began, "you probably know a good deal about me—most of it bad, no doubt——" Here there was laughter and scattered applause. "But few of you, I dare say, have guessed the most interesting thing about me—that I am one of the world's most famous magicians."

More laughter, mingled with catcalls and cries of "Prove it! Prove it!" greeted this statement.

"Yes, prove it!" repeated Freddie, jumping up in excitement.

"Ladies and gentlemen, I will," said Eric gravely.

Before the astonished eyes of his audience, he proceeded to pull a rabbit, an outraged clucking hen and a toy dog out of a tall hat without any trouble at all.

"Do some more," begged the little Bobbsey boy, but Eric said he couldn't just then.

Freddie, disappointed, tried to imitate his hero. He reached for the hat, lost his balance and upset a plate of melted ice-cream all over his best party suit!

While Mrs. Bobbsey was trying to clear up this mess an unexpected visitor was announced. The King of the Carnival had come with his relative, Mrs. Comstock to call on the Bobbsey twins, so all but Freddie went to the lounge to greet them.

"I've brought you a present," the woman smiled, after some handshaking.

When the children unwrapped the big package, they found to their joy that it contained a model of the Ice Palace at Fairy Lake. It was complete to the last detail.

"Oh, what a lovely way to remember our trip here!" cried Nan. "Thank you very much."

When the pretty gift had been exclaimed over by everyone and Mrs. Comstock thanked again and again, Bert asked the lady if she had heard anything about her stolen handbag and diamond ring.

"No," she said, "the police haven't turned up the slightest clue so far."

Then Bert told of seeing the worthless Beany in the cinema that very afternoon. Mrs. Comstock was interested and promised the boy a really fine reward if he could find the thief.

Mrs. Bobbsey came in just then with the cleaned-up Freddie. She was introduced to Mrs. Comstock. Soon afterwards the older people left for the Hotel Windham where there was to be a gala entertainment and ball for the grown-ups. Mr. and Mrs. Bobbsey took Shirley with them.

Left in Aunt Sallie's charge, the tired twins were glad enough to climb into bed. They had not been there long when Nan was awakened by the sound of angry voices outside her door. Running into the hall, she found Mrs. Pry in heated conversation with one of the chambermaids who had left when James Riley had.

"You made me lose my job," this woman berated poor deaf Aunt Sallie. "And I can't get another one, either. I'll have the law on you, that I will!"

"I didn't discharge you. You walked out of your own accord," said Mrs. Pry firmly. "That's not to say you didn't deserve to be fired," she added severely, "for a lazier, more worthless lot of servants than you all were I never did see."

The chambermaid became so angry at this that Nan was really alarmed for Aunt Sallie's safety. She slipped into her room and called the night porter downstairs. The man answered at once. In a moment the watchman appeared. Quietly but firmly he led the troublemaker downstairs and out of the hotel.

Mrs. Pry was very much shaken by the encounter. It was some time before Nan could calm her and persuade her to take some rest.

"I suppose I wasn't meant to be a hotel owner," said the poor lady, shaking her head sadly. "All these troubles are just too much for me. I must see my lawyer first thing in the morning and tell him he must sell the place for me. I want to get back to Lakeport."

"We'll see what we can do to help you," said Nan, and was very thoughtful as she climbed back into bed.

The next day the costumes which the children were to wear as attendants to the King and Queen arrived.

Much excited, the twins ran up to Mrs. Bobbsey's room to try them on.

"Oh, look, aren't they beautiful?" cried Flossie, opening a package and drawing out twin white suits for herself and Freddie. "And look at the hats! Quick, let's put them on!"

When the little children were dressed in identical costumes, they looked more twin-like than ever. As they stood before the mirror, side by side, it was hard to tell which was Freddie and which was Flossie!

Freddie was so interested in his reflection that he pushed forward to get a better view. In so doing he knocked over and broke one of his mother's most expensive bottles of perfume. Even worse than that, the perfume spilled all over the wig that Bert was to wear as page-boy to the King!

"Oh, Freddie, Freddie, I don't know what I shall do with you!" cried Mrs. Bobbsey, rushing to snatch up the wig and save what she could of her perfume. "Why must you be so clumsy?"

"I didn't mean to do it, Mother. I just slipped," said the little boy sadly.

"I know, dear, but not meaning to do it doesn't help much after the damage is done," said his mother. "I'll be glad when my responsibilities for this Ice Carnival are over."

"I'll smell like a perfume shop," complained Bert in disgust. "A fine page-boy I'll be."

"I think the wig will air out, dear," said Mrs. Bobbsey soothingly. "It will be all right by the day of the show, I'm sure. And, anyway, you'll be outdoors where no one will notice it."

In her heart the children's mother was beginning to wish that the Ice Carnival was safely over. So much could happen before then, she thought, especially with Freddie around!

Then something did happen, but it had nothing to do with Freddie. A couple of days later the children were climbing a trail high above Fairy Lake. Presently they heard voices and laughter. Then they came upon a group of men and women building a huge snowman.

The Bobbseys paused to watch. One of the men, recognizing the twins, reached down and swung Flossie up high, until she was seated securely in the arms of the huge white figure.

Now the little girl was not altogether sure that she liked this lofty perch. But everyone else seemed pleased and took it as a joke, so she decided to laugh with the rest.

"Someone ought to take her picture," said one of the women standing near by.

Bert took out his mouth-organ and played a lively tune. The grown-ups joined hands and rollicked around the snowman, shouting out the merry tune. Flossie sang, too, beating time with her mittened hands.

In the midst of this fun a wild cry rang out. Down the trail, out of control and charging straight towards them, galloped a runaway horse!

"Oh, look out!" cried several people.

Bert jumped for the dangling reins. One of the men caught the animal's bridle, slowing the frightened beast to a standstill.

"Help! Help!" came a cry up the trail.

Everyone in the group rushed off to rescue the thrown rider and find out how badly he might have been hurt. Some distance along the trail they came upon him. He had been thrown from his horse into a snowdrift at the side of the trail. Buried almost to his neck in it, he sat there and continued to yell for help.

The unfortunate rider was Danny Rugg!

Meanwhile, no one thought of poor Flossie, perched high in the snowman's arms, unable to get down.

CHAPTER XXI

FLOSSIE'S ADVENTURE

IT was some time before Flossie began to be frightened. She settled herself more comfortably on her cold perch and watched the trail. Every moment she expected to see Nan, Bert, or Freddie come around the curve.

Time went on, however, and no one came. Snow began to fall, gently at first, and then in thicker and faster flakes. The shadows were lengthening, too.

"What shall I do if they don't come!" she thought uneasily.

The ground looked a long way off and she hesitated to jump. Still, it would not do for her to stay much longer in the snowman's arms. She was beginning to grow very cold and the flakes were settling thickly over her.

Shivering, Flossie looked once more at the ground below her. There was nothing else to do—she would have to take a chance and jump!

Gritting her teeth and shutting her eyes, the little girl slipped to the edge of her snowy perch and let herself go. She landed with a thud on the trampled snow and toppled over sideways.

"Oh, dear, I've hurt my ankle," she cried aloud. "I wish someone would come and help me."

A moment later Flossie got to her feet and limped along the trail, a lone little figure in the wintry landscape. The snow was falling faster now and it was hard to see ahead. But she was not really frightened. The very next turn, she felt sure, would bring her to her friends.

Meanwhile, Nan and Bert and Freddie had run with the others to rescue Danny Rugg from the snowbank. In the excitement they forgot that Flossie, held high in the arms of the white giant, was unable to get down and follow them.

Danny proved to be more scared than hurt. When pulled out of the snowbank and brushed off, he was found to be all right except for a few bruises and a rather badly wrenched shoulder. You may be sure the boy made the most of his hurts, bawling loudly whenever anyone came near him.

One of the men had brought up the boy's horse. Danny refused to go near the animal, saying it was too wild.

"I'll ride him back to the stable," Bert Bobbsey volunteered.

"Let me go, too," begged Freddie.

There was some objection on the part of the grown-ups to this suggestion. When they saw how gentle the animal had become, however, and how well Bert handled the reins, they consented to let the two boys ride to the stables.

"Giddy-up," said Freddie gleefully.

Eric the Red had ridden up in his car and now offered to give Nan a lift to the hotel.

"Where's the little princess?" he asked, using his special name for Flossie.

Suddenly Nan remembered where she had left her

little sister. She looked about, but the small girl was nowhere in sight.

"Oh, dear, we must get back to the snowman as fast as we can," she said to Eric. "Please hurry. I suppose Flossie couldn't get down. I'm afraid she will be dreadfully frightened."

The man chuckled as Nan explained where they had left Flossie. He was not at all alarmed, for he expected to rescue his "princess" in a few minutes and return her in triumph to the Central Palace. He even joked a little about the lucky snowman who had been permitted to hold a real live princess in his arms!

Perhaps it was the snow, which had begun to fall heavily, that made them miss the road. At any rate, it was not long before Nan realized that they had been driving much farther than they should have to reach Flossie.

"I'm afraid we went past our turn. Oh, dear, Flossie *will* be frightened," she said anxiously.

Eric looked for a place in the road wide enough to turn the car.

"These trails are wide enough only for mountain goats," he grumbled, backing cautiously.

As he spoke the rear wheels slipped off the hard-packed trail. The front of the car went up and the back down.

"That's fine!" said Eric the Red. "I knew I'd drive us in a ditch if I tried hard enough. Well, I guess I'll just have to get out and push."

Luckily they were not very far off the road. The young man found several old sacks in the car. These he put under the wheels to give them a grip. Then by pushing, hauling, and coaxing, he finally got the machine out of the ditch and on to the road again.

By this time the snow was falling heavily and it was almost dark. Nan was so worried about Flossie she was almost in tears.

This time, however, they found the right turn. A short drive brought them to the open space before the snowman. Nan jumped out of the car and ran to the shadowy figure.

Then she saw, even in the gathering darkness, that Flossie was no longer in the snowman's arms. The little girl was gone! Nan started to cry but Eric the Red put an arm about her reassuringly.

"Why, that's the best thing that could have happened," he said. "All the time we've been worrying about the little princess she has probably been safe at the Central Palace, worrying about you! Come now, dry your eyes and we'll get back to the hotel just as fast as we can."

But there was no Flossie at the Central Palace. Bert and Freddie had not been worried, for they had thought Flossie was with Nan.

"I knew Eric the Red offered to take you home," said the older boy, "so I thought of course he'd bring Flossie, too."

When Nan told her story the children were in a great state of anxiety. Things were made all the worse by the fact that their parents had gone out with Aunt Sallie on business, so there was no one to tell them what to do.

No one, that is, except Eric the Red. Once again he proved himself a friend in need. The young man said he would rouse the whole place, if necessary, to look for Flossie. Almost everyone at Fairy Lake knew and loved the little girl and would be glad to join in the search, he was sure.

Eric took the worried Bobbsey children in his car and started out to search for Flossie. Presently they met the King and Queen on their way to the Ice Palace to preside over some events there. The young people were very much upset upon hearing the news. They said they would cancel all their engagements and join in the hunt.

The King and Queen were as good as their word. All the events at the Ice Palace were called off, while almost everyone at Fairy Lake promised to look for the lost child.

"We *must* find her soon," said Nan, trying to keep back the tears.

This was not going to be easy to do, for Flossie had become hopelessly lost. Slipping and stumbling along the snowy trail, the little girl trudged on. The snow came down more heavily and the shadows deepened all around her.

She had passed many turns since that first one which she had been sure was all that hid her brothers and sister from view. Still she had not found them.

She was growing cold and her ankle hurt. Once she had to stop for several minutes to rest it, but darkness and fear urged her on again.

"What will happen to me if I have to stay here all night?" she thought.

Now Flossie was as brave as most little girls; perhaps she was even braver than some. For a long time she had tried to tell herself that she would certainly come across her brothers and Nan soon. Anyway, someone would come along in a little while who would take her back to the hotel. But as these things did not happen, she began to be badly frightened.

Trees bordering the trail, which were so friendly

in the day-time, looked ghostly and unkind now. Their branches, weighted with the fresh fall of snow, seemed to reach out for the little girl. One of them, lower than the others, did actually brush her shoulder.

Flossie cried out and tried to run but the snow clogged her feet. She could do no more than struggle along heavily for a little way. Suddenly she stopped.

"What was that!" she asked herself.

Something had moved in the woods! Too frightened to move, Flossie just stood and stared. After a moment the "thing" moved again. With a toss of its head it disappeared into the deeper shadows of the woods.

"It was only a deer," the little twin thought in relief and moved on again.

After what seemed to the little girl a long time of pushing through the snow, she came out on a rocky ledge high on the trail. Below in the valley the lights of the Ice Palace sprang up, one by one. Now Flossie knew that she had been following the wrong trail all the time. Every step she had made had taken her farther and farther from Moosehead and home!

She was very cold and tired now. This snowy ledge high up over the valley seemed the loneliest place in the world to the frightened little girl. The lights of the Ice Palace were very far away, but she must try to reach them, she knew. "Somebody there will take me back to Mother and Daddy," she sighed.

Flossie turned away. As she did so, her foot slipped and she plunged forward into space. It happened so suddenly that there seemed to be no time at all between the slip and the moment when the little girl found herself wedged tightly in a rocky crevice.

The fact that the crevice was there had probably

saved her life, but Flossie did not know that. She kicked and squirmed for all she was worth trying to get herself free.

Suddenly something moved on the ledge below her. The little girl grew very quiet. She waited, scarcely daring to breathe!

CHAPTER XXII

NAN HELPS THE KING

CLOSER and closer came the "something" which had frightened Flossie. It was a very large animal, she could tell. She could hear it sniffing curiously, as though surprised to find a little girl on this ledge so far above the world!

Then suddenly a head with antlers came into view around the edge of rock. Flossie's visitor was a big bull moose!

More alarmed than ever, the little girl began to struggle desperately to get free. Suddenly one of her mittens came off, flew up and hit the moose squarely in the eye!

Now if this surprised Flossie, it surprised the buck still more. After one astonished look the animal shook its head and disappeared!

The Bobbsey girl had to laugh. She couldn't help it. In spite of being cold and hungry and scared, she put back her head and giggled long and loud. The moose had looked so awfully funny!

It was so that Bert and Nan found her a few moments later. They had been searching in the neighbourhood and Flossie's familiar giggle drew them to the spot.

What rejoicing there was, then, with the little girl safe on the trail again. She was hugged first by Nan and then by Bert and Freddie and Eric the Red in turn!

On the way back to the hotel, with Nan's arm around her shoulders and a rug wrapped cosily about her, Flossie told her story. In fact, she told it more than once. Several times during the return trip they were stopped by search-parties and each time the small Bobbsey twin had to tell about her adventure again.

Everyone was overjoyed at the little girl's safe return. By the time they reached the hotel Flossie was beginning to like all the attention. She was almost disappointed when her parents, arriving at the hotel, greeted her as though nothing had happened. And indeed nothing had happened as far as they were concerned.

Mr. and Mrs. Bobbsey had been with Aunt Sallie Pry to see her lawyer. They had very interesting news to tell the children.

"Do you remember the property deed you found in the storeroom trunk the other day?" their mother asked the girls.

The children's faces lighted up when they recalled their discovery of a short time ago.

"As if we could forget it, Mother!" cried Nan.

"Did it say Aunt Sallie was to have a whole lot of money?" asked Flossie, wide-eyed.

"Well, not money, exactly. You see, the deed is to some timber-land," Mrs. Bobbsey explained. "Your father thinks the land may turn out to be very valuable."

"I'm going out to look it over tomorrow," Mr. Bobbsey added. "Like to come along, Bert?"

"I want to go too, Daddy," Freddie put in.

"Not tomorrow," said his father firmly. "This is a business trip. And I've learned from experience," he added with a twinkle in his eye, "that business and Freddie don't mix. No sir, tomorrow you stay right here."

All the little boy's coaxing could not make his father change his mind. Freddie changed from coaxing to sulking and even that had no effect except to win him a scolding from his mother. As a result, when his father and Bert started off early the next morning, Freddie was in a rather naughty frame of mind.

Wandering sulkily about the hotel, the little boy fell to wishing that he could find some new toy; something interesting and unusual that would really be fun to play with. One thing he had been wishing he could do was to fire the pistol of the starter of the races at Fairy Lake.

If he could have such a pistol now, just like the one the man used, he could practise with it and then help at the races. Freddie guessed *that* would make his family sit up and take notice! The more he thought of it, the more interesting the idea became.

Meanwhile, Nan had set off on a secret mission. She was determined to speak privately with the King of the Carnival about something on her mind.

Arriving at the club where Victor Comstock had his headquarters, Nan asked to speak to the young man. She had not guessed this would be so hard. The place was full of reporters and costumiers and other people to see the King.

"I'll wait," she replied to a woman who was taking care of things.

With a picture magazine and a chocolate bar Nan settled herself to wait as patiently as she could. At last the reporters and visitors left. With a pleasant smile Victor Comstock took a chair opposite Nan.

"Thank goodness that's over," he said with a weary sigh. "From all the fuss being made, one might think this was going to be a real coronation. Did you get your costumes all right?" he added.

"Oh, yes, thanks, they're lovely—all but Bert's wig," said Nan.

They laughed together over her story of the broken perfume bottle and the sweet-smelling wig. Then, rather hesitantly and shyly, Nan brought up the matter which had prompted her visit.

"I—I suppose you will be glad when all the fuss is over," she began.

"Well, I will in a way. It's been fun, of course, but I won't be sorry to settle down and really get to work again."

This gave Nan the opening for which she was hoping.

"You—you like it here, don't you?" she said, stealing a glance at him. "I mean the climate is really very nice—and—"

Victor Comstock laughed and settled back in his chair, stretching his long legs before him.

"Now look here, young lady," he teased, "you didn't come all this way just to talk with me about the climate, did you? There's something on your mind. Why not tell me all about it?"

Nan met his teasing, friendly glance and smiled back, a little uncertainly.

"Well—that is—it seemed to be a very good idea when I first thought of it, but I don't know how you will feel about it."

"Suppose you try me," the King encouraged, adding, "I say, do you happen to have another chocolate bar?"

"Oh, yes, I have," replied Nan eagerly.

She felt in her sweater pocket and produced the chocolate. The King accepted it gratefully.

"Thanks. You see, I haven't had breakfast as yet," he said.

There was something about that chocolate bar in the King's hand that overcame Nan's shyness. She began to talk freely about Aunt Sallie Pry and the Central Hotel—which Flossie still insisted must be called the Central Palace. She related some of the troubles that had met them when they first arrived at Moosehead and of the problems they had faced since then.

"But the hotel is really in very good shape now," she added earnestly. "We have had it all cleaned and freshened up and everybody seems to like the meals we serve."

"Yes, I have heard people say they can get better food at the Central now than at the Windham."

"Oh, *have* you? I must tell Aunt Sallie that. She'll love it. But you see," Nan went on, "Mrs. Pry is tired of running the hotel. She says it is really—a man's job—and I——"

"Yes?" said the King encouragingly.

"I thought maybe you would like to buy it," said Nan in a rush.

Victor Comstock sat up straight and looked at the girl hard for a moment. Surprise changed to interest and interest to eagerness as he regarded her. He jumped to his feet and began to pace up and down the room.

"Maybe you have hit upon something," he said.

"If I buy the hotel I can settle down here and that means—more than I can tell you. How much does Mrs. Pry want?" he demanded, stopping before Nan.

"I don't know. But I am sure she would be willing to sell the hotel very reasonably," Nan answered, remembering a conversation she had overheard between her father and Aunt Sallie. "To anyone she really liked, that is."

"Maybe Aunt Eleanor would help me," said the King, still thinking aloud. "She is always giving money for worthy causes and this," he added with a smile for Nan, "is certainly a worthy cause."

He was about to say more when his secretary announced that a reporter from the *Daily Star* was there for an interview. The King was forced to take leave of Nan but he promised to think over her suggestion very carefully.

"I'll let you know my decision in a few days," he said, and added with a rueful smile, "A lot depends on Aunt Eleanor, you know."

Now Nan had planned to go right home from the club. But as she paused on the steps, a daring idea came to her. Why should she not go herself to call on Mrs. Comstock? The rich lady was a good friend of the Bobbsey family. She had invited the children on several occasions to visit her whenever they liked. Now, thought Nan, was the time to go!

CHAPTER XXIII

A FRIENDLY PLOT

IF Nan had thought twice, it is possible she would have lost courage. As it was, she marched straight up to Mrs. Comstock's rooms at the Windham and announced herself to the trim-capped personal maid who appeared. She was taken to a bedroom.

"Nan Bobbsey! What a pleasant surprise!" the wealthy woman greeted her.

The lady was genuinely glad to see the girl and asked her to be seated. She had been trying on a long dress before a full-length mirror.

"Do you like my gown?" she asked, turning slowly so that Nan might admire it from every angle. "It's the one I am to wear at the carnival pageant. I'm to be queen mother, you know."

"It's beautiful," said Nan. "I didn't know you were going to be in the court. I'm so glad, and my brothers and sister will be, too."

The woman picked up a picture hat covered with large grey plumes.

"This goes with the dress," she said. "Would you like to see it on?" she asked.

"Oh, yes, please," replied Nan, and added, "I'm sure you will look lovely on the day of the pageant, Mrs. Comstock."

The queen mother was pleased. After Nan had

admired the carnival clothes, the woman brought out some sparkling jewels she would wear also.

"I should think you would be afraid to have on real ones, for fear they'd be lost or stolen," spoke up Nan.

"That is true," agreed Mrs. Comstock, interested in the good sense of this young girl.

At that moment the maid appeared to lay out certain dresses to be cleaned. As they were brought from the cupboard, Nan thought she had never seen so many lovely things. She exclaimed over them in admiration.

"Here's what I call my hard luck dress," laughed Mrs. Comstock, spreading a lovely blue one over Nan's lap. "The first time I wore it at a dinner the waiter slipped and spilled soup down the front of it."

"Oh, what a shame," said Nan, smoothing the lovely silk. "Couldn't you have it cleaned?"

"I did, but the spot still shows. Would you like to have it?" she added with careless good nature. "Your little sister might use it to make clothes for her dolls."

"I know she'd love it. Thank you so much!" returned Nan. She folded the dress and added, trying to lead up to the real object of her visit, "You enjoy doing nice things for people, don't you?"

"Yes, of course. Though I'm afraid I'm not always as generous as I might be."

Mrs. Comstock looked at her young visitor keenly, as though she sensed something more behind her words. With a friendly smile she leaned over and patted Nan's hand.

"If you want to ask me something, my dear, don't be afraid," she said. "I'll be glad to do anything I can for you. Is one of your family in trouble? Is that it?"

"Oh, no," said Nan, shocked at the notion. "It isn't

my family. Nobody's in trouble, really. But you see
I—that is——"

"There now, let's start at the beginning and take
one thing at a time," said the woman kindly. "You
want me to do something for someone. Is that it?"

"I want you to lend some money to the King so
that he can buy Aunt Sallie Pry's hotel," said Nan
suddenly.

"Good gracious, you mean the Central? And what
does Victor say to all this? Does he want to buy an
hotel?"

Having told so much, Nan knew that she would
have to go on and explain the rest. So, shyly and
scarcely daring to look at her hostess, she mentioned
what had seemed to her to be such a very good idea.

"So you see I thought that if the King should
really buy Aunt Sallie's hotel, everybody would be
happy," she concluded earnestly. "Mrs. Pry could go
back to Lakeport and the King could marry the
Queen——"

"So you have noticed that there's a romance there,
too?" said Mrs. Comstock, laughing. "Well, I dare
say you are right. And Victor likes the plan of buying
the hotel, you think?"

"Oh, I'm sure he does, very much!" said Nan.

The King's aunt looked thoughtful. She lifted the
phone and gave the operator a number.

"We'll soon know. I'll have a talk with him," she
said, smiling at Nan.

The conversation that followed was rather one-
sided as far as Nan was concerned. She judged,
though, that Victor was leaving no doubt in the
woman's mind of his enthusiasm for Nan's suggestion.

"He wants to buy it," smiled Mrs. Comstock as she hung up the telephone. "You are a good child," she added, as the girl rose to go. "I'll think over what you have said and let you know my decision just as soon as I've had another talk with Victor. Thank you for coming to me."

"Thank *you*," said Nan fervently. She hesitated, then reached up and gave her friend a shy little kiss. "Thank you—for everything," she said.

Nan walked home to the Central Palace in a happy daze. Her venture had turned out much better than she had dared to hope!

Mrs. Bobbsey listened with interest when her daughter told of the two calls she had made. Her mother suggested that nothing should be said to Mrs. Pry about the possible sale of the hotel until matters should be more definite.

"It would be a shame to raise her hopes and then have to disappoint her," she said.

They were just sitting down to luncheon when Bert and Mr. Bobbsey returned. The two were in the best of spirits and demanded to see Aunt Sallie at once. Not a bite would they eat, they said, until they had told her the good news!

So the old lady was brought from the kitchen where she had been attending to the desserts. She was coaxed to sit down at the Bobbseys' table.

"We've news for you, Aunt Sallie," Bert began.

"Views! I haven't time to listen to any views, or to look at 'em, for that matter," said the deaf woman tartly.

"News, Aunt Sallie, *good news, great news*!" said Mr. Bobbsey, putting a hand on the old lady's arm. "It's about that timber-land of yours."

Mrs. Pry grew quite still, while she looked steadily at the children's father.

"You said—good news?" she whispered.

"The very best, Aunt Sallie. Your land is valuable; some of the best trees I've seen in a long time. Why, you could sell for cash any day. It's as good as money in the bank!"

Tears welled up in Aunt Sallie's eyes and her lips quivered. She turned her face away, pretending to search for a handkerchief. As Nan slipped one into her hand, the old lady said severely:

"I'm not crying, you understand. I—I've just got a cold in my head."

This did not fool the twins at all. Even Flossie and Freddie knew that Aunt Sallie was crying for joy over Mr. Bobbsey's good news.

"She'll never have to worry about money again," said Bert later.

That afternoon the twins again went over to watch the contests at the lake. A great many skiers and skaters had been beaten in previous matches, so now only the best of them remained to compete in the finals. These were to take place on the following day. As Mr. Kape, Shirley Swift, and Eric the Red were in the finals, the twins were looking forward to the morrow with the keenest interest.

For some time they watched the skiers practising their jumps, then wandered off to the part of the lake reserved for visitors. There they found Danny Rugg about to start out alone in his ice-boat.

"Yeah!" he jeered at sight of the Bobbseys. "Bet you'd be afraid to race me again!"

"Bet we wouldn't. We'll give you a race any time you say," retorted Bert.

"How about right now?" Danny challenged.

"Now it is!" returned the Bobbsey boy cheerfully. "Come on, twins, let's show Danny what real ice-boat sailing is like!"

"You bet! Hurrah!" shouted Freddie.

Now the twins had had considerable practice in ice-boat sailing since that first day with Eric the Red. The young man had given them permission to use his craft whenever he did not want it himself. Also he had given them instructions in the best way to handle it. So now they took up Danny's challenge joyfully, confident that they could beat him.

The bully did not wait for a fair start, but shot out ahead of the twins. Bert, dodging other boats at the starting-point, found himself two good lengths behind Danny by the time he reached the open lake. The Rugg boy had the wind in his sails and was scudding along at a good clip.

"Our best chance is to get to lee of him," yelled Bert. "Here, Nan, watch the sail for a minute while I take the tiller. Whoops! Here we go!"

The boat swung around in a wide arc. Danny looked behind, saw what they were about to do and tried to cut across their path. But he turned too sharply. Out bellied the sail with a sound like the snap of a whip and over went the boat.

Danny went down under the flapping canvas!

CHAPTER XXIV

LUCKY SNOWBALL

OF course the Bobbseys won the race. Now Danny would have an added grudge against them!

The twins were having too much fun to care. They continued the sail and on the way back stopped for a time to watch the bobsled races. One of the men, a champion and a friend of Eric the Red, asked the children to take a ride with him.

"Gee, that would be wonderful," said Bert.

Half fearfully the others consented, for the course was a steep and dangerous one. They had often watched the whizzing sleds with a fascination mixed with awe.

They climbed aboard and hung on tightly as they left the starting-platform. Down the snowy track they swooped.

Flossie shrieked with glee. Freddie shouted himself hoarse as they dashed between hard-packed snowy banks and flew around corners at a fearful speed. Nan and Bert yelled, too, but with sheer delight. The keen wind whipped their faces apple-red and their eyes shone with the joy of swift motion.

"This is the best fun I ever had," said Freddie as they got off at the end of the run.

The little boy scooped up a handful of snow and began to roll it into a ball.

"We must get back to the ice-boat," said Bert, after thanking their kind friend for the ride.

Freddie followed the others at a run, holding the melting snow in his hand. When they reached the edge of the lake, the little boy opened his hand to brush away the rest of the snow.

What a surprise!

In the palm of his hand lay something which caught the rays of the sun and winked up at him brightly. It was a beautifully set diamond ring!

Freddie's brother and sisters were even more excited than the little boy over the discovery. They all agreed that the best thing to do was to get back to the hotel just as soon as possible and turn the valuable jewellery over to their parents for safe keeping.

When they reached the Central, they found that Mrs. Comstock had come to call on them. She was talking earnestly to their parents and Aunt Sallie.

When Freddie burst in with his find the King's aunt gave a joyful cry. She took the diamond ring from the little boy's hand and held it up to the light.

"It's my ring—the one I lost the other day when that horrible man stole my handbag," she said. "I'd know it anywhere by the setting. And see, it has my initials inside! Freddie Bobbsey, come here and let me hug you! I never was so glad of anything as I am to get back this ring!"

Freddie came forward a little shyly. He hoped Danny Rugg would not see him being hugged—even by Mrs. Comstock, whom he liked very much!

After embracing him, the visitor put an arm about Nan. She made the girl sit down close to her.

"You know, I really came to see you today," she

confided. "I wanted to talk to you about the conversation we had. Remember?"

"Oh, yes," said Nan eagerly. "Is it—do you——"

"It is and I do!" laughed Mrs. Comstock. "To make a long story short, I have decided to lend Victor the money he needs to buy this hotel; that is," with a glance at Aunt Sallie, "if Mrs. Pry is still willing to sell."

"Oh, that is wonderful!" the girl cried. "It will make so many people happy."

Aunt Sallie was a little confused, at first, as she had not been able to hear all the conversation. When she realized that the hotel was to be sold to a reliable customer, her joy knew no limits. She tried to tell the twins and Mrs. Comstock how she felt, but in the midst of it her voice broke and her eyes filled with tears. As Mrs. Pry fumbled for her handkerchief, Flossie spoke comfortingly to the visitor.

"It's all right," she said. "Aunt Sallie always cries when she's happy."

"I'm not snappy," sniffed the deaf old lady. "I never felt less snappy in my life!"

This made everybody laugh, including Aunt Sallie herself. So it was in a very happy frame of mind that the twins prepared for the Great Day of the carnival.

As they put on their costumes to go to the Ice Palace for a final dress rehearsal, they agreed that there was only one thing needed to make them completely happy. This was to catch Beany Ferris and recover Mrs. Comstock's handbag from the thief. The older twins teased Freddie a little over being such a bad detective.

"Seems as if you should have found Beany by this

time," said Bert. "What kind of a detective are you, anyway?"

"Well, I've sort of forgotten about Beany," Freddie admitted, adding hopefully, "Maybe I'll catch him yet."

Privately the little boy thought that the only way he could ever catch the bad man would be to scare him in some way. But just how to do this he did not know at the moment.

"Come on," called Mr. Bobbsey to the twins. "It's getting late."

Off the children dashed and soon joined the other members of the court. Flossie was so overcome with the dazzling beauty of it all that she could hardly pay attention to the producer.

The dress rehearsal was a great success, however. When the children went to bed, tired but happy, they hoped fervently for a clear day on the morrow.

"Hurrah! The sun is out!" cried Freddie when he opened his eyes the next morning.

Never had a clearer or more beautiful day greeted the Bobbseys since their arrival at Fairy Lake. Certainly it would not be the fault of the weather if the final day of the carnival was not a great success!

Everybody was happy and excited. The little twins could scarcely wait until it was time to dress up in their party costumes. As a result, they were ready to the last button and hook-and-eye long before it was time to start.

Nan, they agreed, looked "perfectly lovely". She wore a long flowing blue dress in which she was to present the King and Queen with the Diamond Key to the Ice Palace.

When Mr. Bobbsey brought the car round to the

door at last, it was found that Bert had no wig. He had put it outside his bedroom window for a final airing, and had almost gone off without it!

At last the twins were really in the car and on their way to Fairy Lake. A few minutes later they took their places in the procession. The gaily decorated sleigh floats were to wind slowly about the lake and come to a stop at the gates of the Ice Palace.

"Oh!" exclaimed Flossie, "look at the Queen!"

The children thought they had never seen anyone as lovely. The beautiful girl was dressed from head to foot in a sparkling white robe. On her head was a crown studded with gleaming jewels.

The King looked very handsome, too. He was so splendid in his royal robes and a sceptre in his hands that Nan wondered if he weren't really a king. How had she ever had the courage to ask him to buy Aunt Sallie's hotel! When the King caught her eye, however, he smiled and winked at her—by which Nan knew that he was only a very nice young man named Victor Comstock, after all!

At last everyone was in place. To the blare of trumpets the royal procession started. Then the band music began.

"Isn't this fun?" cried Flossie.

"Sh!" said Freddie, "you are s'posed to be dig'ified."

So the Bobbsey twins rode around the lake, looking very proud, as became members of the court. The King and Queen acknowledged the cheers of the onlookers with courtly bows and now and then a wave of the hand. But Freddie and Flossie looked straight ahead with their haughty little noses in the air.

"Bert makes a fine page," thought Nan proudly.

Her twin did look well in his short flared tunic and pointed medieval shoes. The others did not know that the boy was in torment over his wig, for fear someone would think he had put perfume on it on purpose!

All around the lake the parade went with the music playing and the people cheering. At the proper time Nan dropped out of the group and waited for the others at the gates of the palace. She came forward to present the large Diamond Key to the King.

The other Bobbsey children were very proud of their sister. They could see how everyone admired her as she made her little speech and presented the key in her own sweet, gracious way.

Then, amid shouts and applause from the crowd and a salute from the starter's gun, the King and Queen entered the Ice Palace, followed by the courtiers. As they went through the gorgeously decorated gateway Bert and Nan heard the King say:

"You will marry me, won't you, Janet?"

Unfortunately a burst of music from the orchestra within the palace drowned out the Queen's reply. They could only guess what she had answered.

When the King and Queen and the other members of the court were seated in the royal box, the entertainment on the indoor rink began. It was wonderful to watch, especially the skating figures done to music.

After a while Freddie became a little bored. No one noticed when he wandered off in search of other amusement.

He went along a hallway of the club-house, which was behind the Ice Palace, until he found himself at last in a rather large room. It was filled with suitcases and clothing of all sorts. It seemed to be a combination storage- and dressing-room. What caught Freddie's eye was a man's costume made of silver cloth with a wide metal belt studded with coloured stones. Best of all was the gleaming silver pistol in the belt's holster.

"That's better than the King's costume," thought Freddie, excited at his find.

Suddenly there was a sound behind him. The little boy turned in time to see a figure climb through the window and drop noiselessly to the floor. It was Beany Ferris!

Freddie looked at the pistol. He knew that it was just a fake, but Beany did not know this! Now was the little boy's chance to scare the thief and capture him!

CHAPTER XXV

BEANY IS CAUGHT

FREDDIE BOBBSEY picked up the pistol in both hands. As he did so it was turned right towards Beany!

At that moment the man saw the lad and leaped at him. Freddie felt the gun being twisted from his hands. In his effort to hold on to it, he must have touched the trigger.

Bang!

The pistol went off with a loud report and Beany Ferris dropped it. He kicked it away with his foot, so that it landed under the table.

At the same instant the door opened. Nan, Bert, and Flossie rushed into the room.

"I've got Beany!" shouted Freddie, too excited to tell the exact truth. "Hold on to him so he won't get away."

That's just what Nan and Bert were doing. Flossie tried to help but all she could get hold of was one end of Beany's coat! The man was pulling towards the window.

"Help! Help!" the twins shouted.

The children's cries soon brought help. The thief, snarling and ugly, was held by several men. The police were called and promised to "get the truth out of the fellow" before the night was over. Then they took him to jail.

Meanwhile, the Kapes and Mrs. Comstock were told of the capture. At once they went down to see the prisoner, promising to meet the Bobbseys later at the hotel.

Freddie found himself something of a hero, although Mrs. Bobbsey made him promise he never would touch other people's things again, especially pistols! As a matter of fact, Freddie was glad enough to make the promise, for the gun going off so close to him, had frightened him rather badly!

After a delicious supper at the club-house, the Bobbsey children were allowed to stay for the evening events. They even went with the King and Queen afterwards to enjoy the fireworks which were to wind up the celebration.

Flossie, finding herself beside the Queen, snuggled close to the beautiful young woman. She reached up and pulled the young woman's head down to hers.

"You *are* going to marry the King and live at the Central Palace for ever and ever, aren't you?" she asked.

"Yes," smiled the pretty Queen, "I am."

This made a perfect ending to the holiday of the Bobbsey twins. Everybody was happy, thought the children: Mr. and Mrs. Kape because they were able to get back the articles stolen from their burned house; Mrs. Comstock because her handbag, pearls, and railway ticket were returned to her. Unfortunately the seventy-five dollars had been spent by Beany before his arrest.

Aunt Sallie was happy because the hotel had been sold at a fair price. And her timber-land promised to bring more money than even Mr. Bobbsey had hoped for.

It went without saying that the King was more than happy. As for the Queen—there was no need to wonder about her. One could tell, just by looking at her, how she felt!

"Come to think of it, I imagine the only person who isn't joyful is Beany Ferris," said Nan, busy packing her things for the return to Lakeport.

"I suppose that can't be helped," said her mother. "A thief just has to be punished."

The next day, loaded with souvenirs and carrying the good wishes of all their friends at Fairy Lake, the Bobbseys and Aunt Sallie Pry took the train for home. The Kapes and the Ruggs went too. Now the twins were glad of the Kapes' company, but they could have done without Danny's very easily!

The King and Queen, Eric the Red, and Shirley Swift came down to the station to bid them good-bye. Shirley and Nan clung together and sighed a little at the parting.

"I hope we'll meet again," said the Bobbsey girl, her eyes filling with tears, for she had grown very fond of her new friend.

"I'll surely come to see you," Shirley promised.

Danny Rugg, shoving through the crowd, saw them and sneered aloud.

"Isn't that just like girls?" he said to his mother. "Always sniffing and blubbering in public."

"Hush, dear," his mother replied, looking embarrassed. "One of those girls is Shirley Swift, the famous skater. I wish you would get her to give you her autograph. It would be something to show the folks at home."

Danny, urged on by his mother, approached Shirley to ask her. The young star was just putting her name on a picture which she intended as a present to Nan.

"Please, will you——" began the boy.

Shirley gave him one freezing look and turned her back. "Sorry, but I never sign my name except for my friends!" she said.

Then there was a lot of bustle and excitement as the train came in. The King picked up Flossie and kissed her and then handed her over to Mr. Bobbsey. He shook hands with Bert and Freddie and then turned to Nan. He had saved his farewell to her for the last, he said, because he owed her a special debt.

"You've done me the biggest favour ever," he said sincerely.

So Nan was kissed by a King and hugged by a Queen and both told her how grateful they were to her.

"Come back soon! You will always find a welcome at the Central Palace," they called.

Then the train began to move and through misted eyes Nan and Flossie saw the station slip away.

"I hope we can come back again some time," said the older girl wistfully. "We had such a lovely holiday at Fairy Lake!"

"The best one we ever had!" exclaimed her sister.

For some reason the trip home seemed much faster than the one going up. Perhaps this was because there was no blizzard to retard them now. Or perhaps it was because Mr. Kape entertained them with stories and by bringing out all the prizes he had won at the carnival. They certainly looked very bright and shiny spread out in a row.

Freddie said that some day he hoped to be as fine

a skater as Mr. Kape. The man promised to give him some lessons on the pond when they were back in Lakeport.

"It will seem like a very little pond after Fairy Lake," said Freddie dolefully.

"But plenty big enough to tumble down on," laughed Mrs. Bobbsey.

At last the journey was over. The train rolled into the Lakeport station and the Bobbseys found Sam waiting for them in the family car. They were to keep Aunt Sallie with them for a day or two until she was rested from the trip. They urged the Kapes to come home with them, too, if only for the night.

Mr. Kape hesitated. "We have rented a furnished house, you know, until our own can be rebuilt."

"Yes, perhaps we'd better go right there," said his wife a little uncertainly.

"Nonsense! You will come right home with us and have a hot dinner and a comfortable place to sleep," said Mrs. Bobbsey in the tone which, as the children well knew, meant she was not to be denied. "Dinah will be delighted to have you. She loves company."

So in the end Mrs. Bobbsey had her way. The car was very crowded, but no one minded for such a short distance.

The house looked cheerful and homey when they reached it. There was a light on the porch to welcome them and a moment later the door was opened by Dinah. Waggo barked and jumped around joyfully. Even old Snap came out to greet them.

As the children tumbled into the warmth and cheer of the hall they were glad to be home. It was such a pleasant home.

"I'se right glad to see yo' chilluns back," said

Dinah, grinning broadly. "I done make something I thought yo' all would like for supper."

"Um-yum!" said the twins and made a dash for the dining-room.

Suddenly they all heard a new sound. A canary was singing!

"Ah thought mebbe yo' would like music with yo' meals," said Dinah, "especially now dat yo' is members of de court of a King and Queen," she laughed.

The children said together dear old Dinah was wonderful and so different from some of the servants they had met at first at the Central Hotel.

As everyone was about to sit down, Bert looked at his twin. "Gee," he said, "Fairy Lake sure was a great place."

"But not as good as this one, just the same," added Nan happily.